BEING HERS

ANNA STONE

Cover by Kasmit Covers

ISBN: 978-0-64841-921-1

CHAPTER ONE

Smooth, bass-heavy pop music pulsed through the room. The patrons drank, danced, and lounged on plush chairs under glittering lights. Gorgeous women adorned in diamonds and designer dresses flirted with rich businessmen in Italian suits. B-list celebrities flaunted their wealth, throwing away wads of cash on two thousand-dollar bottles of champagne.

Mel walked over to a table occupied by a young woman and a man who looked old enough to be her grandfather. She cleared the empty glasses from the table. "Can I get you anything else?"

"Another bourbon on the rocks," the man said, not bothering to look up at her. "And another of those fruity things for her."

"Coming right up." Luckily for him, Mel remembered what cocktail that 'fruity thing' was.

Mel returned to the bar and relayed the drink order to the bartender. She plucked a soggy napkin from the bottom of her shoe. Just another night at The Lounge. Part high-end bar, part nightclub, it was one of the city's most exclusive night spots. Or so she was told. When she wasn't working, Mel spent most of her nights at home or at the library, writing papers and combing through law textbooks.

Mel delivered the drinks to the couple on a silver tray, then took another order. She went back and forth, serving drinks and wiping down tables until her feet ached and her muscles burned. Mercifully, by that time her shift was almost over.

"Hey, Mel?" James, her manager, beckoned her over to the bar.

"What's up, James?" Mel leaned down on the bar, grateful for a moment to catch her breath. She'd spent the whole day in classes and had been on her feet all night.

"Here." James handed her a large envelope. "It's your new contract."

"Does this mean I'm off probation?" Mel flicked through the pages. Everyone who worked at The Lounge started on a probationary period due to the clientele's high standards. The patrons expected nothing short of the royal treatment, and they did not tolerate mistakes. Mel had never worked at a club before starting at The Lounge, but she was a fast learner.

"Yep. I recommended you for a permanent position weeks ago, but I've been waiting for the owner's approval. He likes to have the final say in everything."

Mel found that surprising. The identity of The Lounge's owner was a complete mystery. No one seemed to know who he was, and none of the staff had ever met him. As the manager, James was the exception, but all he would tell anyone was that the owner was an extremely private person.

Mel signed the contract and handed it back to James.

"Congratulations, you're one of us now," he said.

"Thanks." Mel breathed a sigh of relief. A little job security was a huge weight off her shoulders.

"By the way, a few of us are going out for drinks after we close. Want to come?"

"Thanks, but I have a paper to finish." It was one of her standard answers. A paper to finish, an exam to prepare for, some supplemental reading to do.

"Come on, Mel. You're always here or at law school. Do you ever do anything fun?"

"I go running sometimes."

"That doesn't count."

"I have a social life. Really." Mel didn't mention that her 'social life' mostly involved going to law school networking events.

"Okay. But you're missing out. If you think the crowd at The Lounge is wild, you should see us after a few drinks."

"Maybe next time," Mel said.

James grinned. He wasn't a bad guy. For a manager, he was extremely laid-back. James was in his late twenties, and he treated his staff like friends. This included Mel, despite her constantly knocking back his invitations to come out for drinks. She hoped he didn't have an ulterior motive. It wouldn't be the first time a guy didn't realize that he was barking up the wrong tree.

James pushed a tray toward her. It held a single glass of whiskey. "Can you take this to table six?"

"Sure." Mel grabbed the tray and edged past the crowd.

Table six was at the far corner of the room. As the crowd thinned in front of her, Mel's heart skipped a beat.

It was her.

She sat alone, upright in her chair as if it were a throne. She wore an ivory silk dress that clung to her slender curves. Her jet black hair cascaded down her shoulders in loose, perfect waves, and her blue eyes were framed by long, dark lashes.

The woman was a regular at The Lounge, coming in around once a week. She always came alone and sat at that table by herself, watching the crowd but never speaking to anyone. Unlike all the other regulars, none of the staff knew anything about her. Not her name, not her job, not how she made her riches. And she had to be rich to afford to come to a place like The Lounge. All that Mel knew about her was that she always drank the same brand of top-shelf whiskey.

As Mel walked toward the woman's table, she was cut off by a sharply dressed man in a suit. He'd had more than a few drinks. He leaned down toward the woman and flashed her a pearl-white smile, then said something to her that Mel couldn't make out.

The woman gestured for the man to lean down closer. She whispered something into his ear. Slowly, his face turned redder and redder. Then without another word, he stood up and scurried off.

Mel watched the man depart. What did the woman say to him? When Mel turned back to her table, the woman was staring straight at her.

"Enjoy the show?" the woman asked.

"I..." Mel trailed off, flustered. She had never spoken to

the woman before, beyond taking her orders and serving her drinks. "What did you say to him?"

"He tried to impress me with his name and his job. And he had some rather vulgar words for me. I told him my name, and that he should pray that we never cross paths out in the corporate world, because after speaking to me like that, I would make sure that no one does business with him again."

Who was this woman that she could intimidate a man with nothing more than her name and some harsh words? Mel remembered the tray in her hands. "Your drink." She placed the glass of whiskey on the table.

"Thank you." The woman's velvet voice sent a shiver careening down the back of Mel's neck.

"Can I get you anything else?"

The woman didn't answer immediately. She picked up her drink, swirled it around and took a sip, leaving a red lip print on the rim of the glass. She placed it down on the table before her. "No. Thank you."

Mel lingered at the table. She was intrigued by this woman. It wasn't just that Mel found her irresistibly attractive. There was something different about her. On the surface, she undeniably belonged to the elite. From her stylish clothing down to her short, manicured fingernails, everything about her pointed to someone accustomed to a life of luxury. But she made no effort to flaunt her wealth and showed none of the entitlement of the other customers.

"Is there something else?" the woman asked.

Mel paused. She felt compelled to ask the woman something, anything. "Why do you come here?" The words tumbled out of Mel's mouth. "It's just that... you're always by yourself, and you don't seem to want to talk to anyone."

The woman leaned back in her chair and studied Mel's face. "You've been watching me."

Mel's face grew hot. She tucked a stray lock of her brown hair behind her ear.

"I like to watch people too," the woman said. "That's why I come here. And to enjoy the fine selection of whiskey that The Lounge has on offer." Her eyes never leaving Mel's, she picked up her glass and took another long sip.

Mel stood there, held captive by the woman's gaze. Her heart raced. There was something in her eyes that Mel couldn't quite decipher. Flirtation? An invitation?

A command?

A raucous shout from somewhere behind her broke Mel out of her trance. "I should go. Let me know if you need anything else."

The woman nodded, her expression inscrutable. As Mel walked away, she swore that she could feel the woman's eyes on her back.

Mel pulled herself together and made her way back to the bar. She was probably imagining things. Mel doubted that the woman even remembered her, considering how many servers worked at The Lounge.

"Mel, can you take these to the VIP section?" James handed Mel a tray holding two bottles of top-shelf champagne and half a dozen crystal flutes.

"Sure." Mel gritted her teeth. There were two ways that a customer could get into the VIP section. One was fame. That got them in for free. The second was money. So much money that even the regular patrons couldn't afford it.

Serving in the VIP section meant big tips; however, VIPs tended to be far more demanding. Mel had quickly learned how to deal with difficult customers, but that made it no less stressful.

Mel made her way through the crowd, balancing the tray carefully in her hands. The contents were worth more than her entire bank account. She couldn't help but feel nervous about toting a small fortune in fragile glass in a crowded room.

She climbed the steps up to the VIP area. A group of men were seated around the table. As Mel approached them, one of them let out a drunken cheer. *Great, frat bros in suits.* As she reached the table, another man stood up and swiveled toward her. His arm hit the tray in Mel's hands and it fell to the floor with a loud crash, leaving Mel standing in a puddle of champagne and broken glass. She cursed under her breath.

"What the fuck?" The hulking man leapt back.

"I'm sorry, sir," Mel said as politely as she could manage. He was the one who had knocked everything out of her hands. But she wasn't about to argue with him. She grabbed the dish towel from her apron and tried in vain to contain the spill.

"Look. Look at my shoes!" The man waved his foot in front of Mel's face. There was a tiny spot on his suede shoe. It could have been anything. "Do you have any idea how much these cost?" His face was bright red.

Mel stood up. "I'm sorry. Let me go get-"

He grabbed her arm and pulled her toward him. "Sorry isn't good enough."

Mel froze. His clammy hand felt like a vice around her

arm. She could smell the cigarettes and alcohol on his breath. Before she could react, a voice rang out from behind the man.

"Take your hands off her. Now."

The man released Mel. She looked over his shoulder. It was the woman in the ivory dress from earlier. She had her hand on the man's shoulder and a look on her face that sent a chill down Mel's spine.

"Get out," the woman said, her voice cold and clear. "And take your friends with you."

The man looked her up and down. "Who the hell are you?"

"I'm the owner of this establishment."

Mel's eyes widened. *She* was the owner of The Lounge?

The man scoffed and looked over at his friends. They averted their eyes and shifted in their seats. He looked back at the woman. "You own this place?"

"That's right. Get out of my club. Now."

The woman stared at the man, her face set like stone. He stared back at her, eyes narrowed. He was easily twice her size, but she held his stare.

Finally, the man looked away. "Like I'd want to stay in a place like this anyway," he mumbled. He turned to his friends. "Let's get out of here."

He grabbed his jacket and walked off toward the door. The others filed out after him, looking sheepish and apologetic. The woman watched them leave, a dark look on her face. As soon as they were out the door, she turned back to Mel.

"Come with me."

CHAPTER TWO

The woman placed her hand on Mel's arm and guided her toward the back of the club. Mel's head was spinning. All this time, the woman had never given any indication that she was anything but another customer. And Mel wasn't sure how to feel about being 'rescued.' She wasn't some helpless damsel. Mel could have dealt with the customer herself, yet she couldn't deny how this woman's hand on her arm sent her pulse racing.

The woman led Mel into a dark corridor tucked away in the corner. As far as Mel knew, all that was down there was a fire exit. To her surprise, there was another door to the right of them that was barely visible in the dim light. The woman opened the door. Mel followed her up a flight of stairs to another door. The woman typed a code into a keypad and the lock on the door clicked open.

Mel followed her into the room. It resembled a generously-sized hotel room, with a large bed at one end and some seating arranged around a coffee table in the center.

With minimalist décor and the clean, sharp angles of the furniture, the space both looked and felt immaculate.

"Sit." The woman gestured toward a leather couch.

Mel sat down. The woman's tone made her wonder if she was in trouble. "Is this about the broken bottles? It was an accident, he-"

"I didn't bring you in here to reprimand you. The loss of a couple of bottles of champagne won't make the slightest dent in the club's profits."

"Oh." That didn't make Mel feel any less restless. "Then why did you bring me back here?"

"I want to make sure you're all right."

"I'm fine," Mel said. "I could have handled it myself," she added.

"I'm sure you could have. Show me your arm."

Mel held her arm out. The woman took Mel's wrist and pulled it closer to the light. The brush of her fingertips against the inside of Mel's wrist made the hairs stand up on her skin.

"Does anything hurt?" The woman inspected Mel's arm.

"No. He didn't grab me very hard."

She released Mel's wrist, apparently satisfied. Her face clouded over. "That man. I'm going to make sure he and his friends never set foot in here again." The woman clenched her fists. "I should have had him arrested for manhandling you like that."

"It wasn't as bad as it looked." Mel wondered if the woman had seen the entire incident, or just Mel standing in a pile of alcohol and glass with a large, angry man's hand around her arm. "He knocked my tray out of my hands by accident and got mad. That's all. I'm used to dealing with difficult customers." Mel was supposed to be serving said customers right now. Had anyone cleaned up all that broken glass? She stood up. "I should get back to work."

"You're not going anywhere until I'm sure you're okay, Melanie."

"I'm *fine*."

"Indulge me then." It was clear that there was no point arguing with her.

Mel sat back down. As she looked around the room, she spotted a few personal items. A silk robe hanging from a hook on the wall. A fluffy white towel on the back of the door to the bathroom. A bottle of whiskey and some glasses on the counter. It was the same whiskey that the woman always ordered downstairs. The space didn't look lived in enough to be more than an occasional hideout, but it was clearly hers.

Mel's eyes wandered over to the bed. As she admired the black satin sheets, something caught her eye.

Hanging from the bedpost was a black leather riding crop with a crimson handle.

Heat rose up Mel's body. For a fleeting moment, an image of the woman wielding the whip played in her mind. She tore her eyes away and pushed the thought out of her head. But she was suddenly hyperaware that she was alone in the room of a domineering woman who she felt an undeniable attraction toward. One who owned a whip.

And that woman was looking straight at Mel.

Mel looked intently down at the hem of her skirt. Had the woman noticed her staring at what was on the bedpost? Mel peeked up at her. Her face gave nothing away.

The woman stood up. "Let me get you a drink." Without

waiting for a response, she walked over to the counter and poured two glasses of whiskey. "Here."

Mel took the proffered glass and drank, wincing as it burned her throat. But the taste wasn't bad.

The woman sat down in an armchair across from Mel. "I take it you're not a whiskey drinker?"

"Nope." The only whiskey Mel had ever tried was cheap stuff that tasted like a campfire.

"Would you like something else?"

"No, this is fine." Mel took another sip. "It actually tastes pretty good."

"It should. This is arguably one of the best whiskeys to come out of Scotland in the last decade or two. It's well worth the price tag."

Mel recalled how much even a single glass of this particular whiskey cost downstairs. For the second time that night, she held a small fortune in her hands, so she figured she may as well enjoy it. Mel sank into the soft couch, her tension clearing. There was a faint floral scent in the air. Rose, and something both sweet and spicy that Mel didn't recognize. She could hear the faint thrum of the music from the club below. It was far softer than it should have been. The room must have been soundproof.

Mel sneaked a glance in the woman's direction. The soft light of the room highlighted her elegant beauty. High cheekbones. Full red lips. Porcelain skin. Her hands had felt so soft on Mel's arm.

Mel suddenly realized that she didn't even know the woman's name. As she opened her mouth to ask, another thought occurred to her. "You called me Melanie earlier. I haven't told you my name."

"There isn't a single person who works here whose name I don't know. And I know more than your name. Melanie Greene, twenty-three years old. Raised by a single mother in a small town in Ohio. Got into college on a full ride scholarship and graduated with honors. Currently studying law. And not even a parking ticket to your name."

"How do you know so much about me?" Mel asked.

"I assure you it's nothing sinister. I require thorough background checks on everyone who works at my establishments before I hire them. I have an excellent memory." She leaned forward and placed her drink on the table. "And you're very hard to forget."

Mel took another sip of her drink. Her glass was emptying quickly.

"You stood out to me, Melanie. It's clear that you have a lot of drive and aren't afraid of hard work. Those are desirable traits to any employer."

Mel remembered her other question. "What's your name?"

"How rude of me. It's Vanessa. Vanessa Harper."

Vanessa. Even her name sounded elegant.

"So, tell me. Why do you want to become a lawyer? You don't seem the type who aspires to work at a big corporate law firm."

Mel would have been bothered by Vanessa's presumption if it hadn't been true. "I want to help those who really need it. For some people, legal services are a luxury they can't afford. Without it, they face poverty, or homelessness, or even prison." Mel knew this well from her own childhood. She grew up in a world that was the complete opposite of the one that Vanessa and the patrons of The Lounge inhabited. "I want to give people like that a chance at a better life."

"How benevolent of you." It was hard to tell whether or not Vanessa was being patronizing. "But you're at one of the top law schools in the country. Simply doing pro-bono work seems like wasted potential."

"I want to do far more than that," Mel replied. "I want to make a difference on a bigger scale. I don't know how exactly yet. But I do know that change comes from the top. And that's why I have to get there."

Vanessa smiled. "You're very passionate. You remind me of myself when I was younger. Big ambitions. Fighting your way up in a world where everything is stacked against you. I can tell you from experience that it isn't easy being a woman in a male-dominated profession. Not to mention a gay woman. Which I'm sure you know already."

Mel almost choked on her drink. "How do you know I'm a lesbian?" She was the kind of woman who flew under most people's gaydar.

"Reading people is one of my talents. I'm an executive. And in the corporate world, it's a valuable skill. Learn someone's tells, and you know when they're lying, or stalling, or when you have them right where you want them. And once you know how to read people, you can learn all sorts of things about someone by simply watching them for five minutes. I've watched you in the club, Melanie. I've watched you interact with people. It's obvious that you're not interested in men, but you are interested in women." Vanessa leaned forward, her eyes locked on Mel's. "And I've seen the way you look at me."

Mel's heart stopped in her chest. The heat of Vanessa's gaze made Mel's skin burn.

She glanced away. Her eyes landed on a clock on the wall. Her shift had ended ten minutes ago.

"I've kept you here long enough," Vanessa said. "You can go." She reached out and took Mel's empty glass from her hand. Their fingers touched, and Vanessa's hand seemed to linger on Mel's. Then Vanessa placed the glass down next to her own and stood up.

Mel got up from the couch, feeling a mixture of relief and disappointment. As she followed Vanessa to the door, her eyes flicked over to the riding crop hanging from the bedpost.

A hint of a smile formed on Vanessa's lips. "Goodbye, Melanie."

CHAPTER THREE

$\mathcal{M}$el jogged down the busy sidewalk, upbeat music blasting through her earbuds. As she narrowly dodged a woman on a bicycle, she wished she could afford a gym membership and avoid the crowded city streets. But for now, she had to make do. Running was her only outlet. She loved the feeling of pushing her body to its limit. The burning muscles. The aching lungs. The high. It was satisfying in a raw, visceral way.

In truth, she preferred the freedom of running outdoors. The heat of the sun on her skin and the wind in her face added to the rush she felt.

Her apartment building came into view. Mel slowed her pace and checked her watch. She didn't have long until she had to leave for work. She'd barely been able to squeeze in a run at all. Wiping the sweat from her brow, Mel jogged the last half mile to her building and made her way up to her apartment. Calling it an 'apartment' was generous. The one-room studio had room for a bed, a table, and little else. But it was the only place that Mel could afford by herself.

She stripped off her sweaty clothes and threw them into the hamper. She'd tried as hard as she could to make her apartment look inviting, adding some color and personal touches. A few throw pillows in a bright, cheerful blue. Posters to cover the marks on the walls. A bookshelf salvaged from the curb that Mel had filled with books she didn't have time to read. It did little to improve the ambiance of the space. But Mel liked it. It was more of a home to her than any other place she had lived in.

Mel made her way to the bathroom and stepped into the shower. She tipped back her head and let the warm water trickle down her body, washing the sweat from her skin and revitalizing her tired muscles. She wished that she had a bathtub. It had been a long day. Six hours of classes, followed by a quick run, and now a shift at The Lounge. She wouldn't get home until well after midnight.

Mel let out a long breath. She was used to it. The long hours. The late nights. The never-ending pile of school work. She'd been working hard since high school: first to get into college and escape her middle of nowhere home-town, and then to get into law school, all while working to support herself.

But as she scrubbed the dirt of the day off her body, Mel felt the weight of it all creep back onto her shoulders. Running provided a brief escape. It didn't last.

She sighed and tried to push it all aside. For what felt like the hundredth time this week, her thoughts drifted back to the other night at The Lounge. To Vanessa. When Mel closed her eyes, she could see Vanessa's smoldering eyes staring back at her. She could feel Vanessa's fingers wrapped around her wrist. She could hear Vanessa's voice, somehow gentle and commanding at the same time.

I've seen the way you look at me.

Mel stepped out of the shower. How had Vanessa managed to get inside her head so easily? It didn't matter. Even if Vanessa was interested in her, which seemed crazy, Mel didn't want to go down that road. Not with Vanessa, or with anyone.

As she toweled herself off, an image of the riding crop hanging from Vanessa's bedpost flashed across Mel's mind. And then, Vanessa holding the crimson handle…

No. Mel refused to let her imagination go there. She left the bathroom and started to get dressed for work.

As soon as Mel arrived at work, James pulled her aside.

"Hey, Mel." His usually cheerful expression had been replaced by one of concern. "How are you doing?"

"I'm fine. What's going on?"

"Vanessa told me about what happened the other night."

Vanessa had told James that she had taken Mel up to her room?

"You know, with that asshole in the VIP area."

Of course. She'd forgotten all about that part of her night. "Right."

"Just so you know, that guy will never set foot in here again. No matter how rich or famous a customer thinks they are, lay a hand on my staff and you're banned for life. He's on Vanessa's blacklist now, which means he's banned from a long list of venues," James said.

"Okay. Thanks, James." Mel paused. "So, you've known about Vanessa all this time?"

"Yep. But I'm not supposed to tell anyone. She has her reasons for keeping her identity private." He held up his hands apologetically. "Don't worry. She doesn't come in here to monitor anyone. She just likes to check up on the place every now and then."

That wasn't particularly reassuring. Would Mel have treated Vanessa any differently all this time if she'd known? It was probably a good thing. Mel didn't need another reason to be intimidated by her.

It turned out to be a quiet night. For what seemed like the twentieth time since her shift started, Mel wiped down an already clean table and rearranged the chairs around it. She ran her fingers through her hair and looked around for something else to do.

"Mel?" James waved her over to the bar. "Want to practice your bartending skills while things are quiet?"

"Sure," Mel replied. James had been training her as a bartender so she could help out when things got busy.

"If you need any help, I'll be right here unpacking these." He pointed to a stack of boxes behind him.

Mel slid behind the bar and began making drinks. She knew most of the cocktail recipes by now, so it was mostly a matter of honing her technique. In between customers, James gave Mel the latest of many informal lessons on bartending. Today, it was about different wines. Mel listened carefully and filed it all away in her mind.

A few minutes before the end of Mel's shift, James pulled a bottle of amber spirits out of a box. The label was written in Japanese. "This must be one of Vanessa's special orders," he said. "Now that you're in on her secret, you can give this to her for me. Here." He held the bottle out to Mel. "She's upstairs looking over some paperwork."

Mel's heart jumped. "Sure thing."

"You might as well head off early. It's dead tonight. Just take it up to her on your way out."

Mel took the bottle from James and grabbed her bag and coat. She said a quick goodbye to her coworkers, then made her way across the club to the corridor that led to Vanessa's room. Her stomach filled with butterflies, she climbed the stairs and knocked on the door.

"It's unlocked," Vanessa called from inside.

Mel entered the room. Vanessa was sitting at the table, her back toward Mel, looking down at some papers spread out before her.

"I need a minute, James-" Vanessa turned her head. She seemed entirely unfazed to see Mel standing in her door-way. "Hello, Melanie."

Usually, Mel didn't like it when people called her by her full name. But it didn't bother her when Vanessa did. "Hi."

"Come in. Sit. I'll be with you in a moment." Vanessa turned back to her work.

Mel sat down on the couch, bottle in hand. She couldn't help but glance over at Vanessa's bed. *Yep.* It was still there. The crimson-handled riding crop.

Vanessa's chair scraped across the floorboards. She gathered her papers and placed them to the side neatly, then walked over to Mel. "What can I do for you?"

"Here." Mel held the bottle out to her. "James asked me to give you this."

Vanessa took the bottle from Mel and held it up in front

of her eyes. "I've been waiting for this. Single malt Japanese whiskey. Aged for thirty years, cask finished. Very difficult to find."

To Mel's surprise, she knew what all of those terms meant. James's lessons had stuck with her. Mel got up to leave.

"Stay. Drink this with me." Vanessa's eyes fell to the coat and purse slung over Mel's arm. "Unless you have somewhere to be?"

Mel hesitated. She did have a lot of work to do. But she wanted to stay. One drink wouldn't hurt. "No, I don't," she said, sitting back down.

Vanessa walked over to the counter. She took two glasses and poured the amber liquid into them, then brought them over to the couch and handed one to Mel. Vanessa took a seat in the chair across from Mel. She swirled the whiskey around in her glass and held it up to her nose. She took a sip. "Not bad," Vanessa declared.

Mel followed Vanessa's lead. She couldn't taste any difference between this whiskey and the one she'd tried the other night.

"So." Vanessa placed her glass down on the table carefully. "Last time you were in here, I ambushed you with questions. Now that I know so much about you, it's only fair that I give you a chance to get to know me. Is there anything you'd like to ask me?"

Mel's mind went blank. There was so much she wanted to know about Vanessa that she didn't know where to start. "*You're* the mystery owner of The Lounge?" It was the only thing she could think of.

"I've heard that I'm quite the mystery to you all. Yes, I

own The Lounge. It's one of quite a few bars and clubs that I own. I moved on to bigger things long ago. But I have a soft spot for this place. It was my first investment." She leaned back in her chair. "You seem surprised."

"A little," Mel said. "Everyone thinks you're some rich old man."

"I assure you I'm not a man, and I'm only thirty-four" Vanessa said. "I haven't done anything to discourage those rumors. I may have even dropped a few hints to throw people off my trail."

"But why the secrecy?" Mel asked.

"A few reasons. I run my own investment firm now. Most of the firm's clients are extremely conservative. And some of the clubs and venues that I own privately could be considered unsavory to some. Not all of them are as respectable as The Lounge. So I don't want them associated with my name and my firm."

What kind of place was less respectable than The Lounge? It wasn't uncommon for Mel to find little white powder smudges on the restroom countertops.

"And quite simply, I'm a very private person. I don't want anyone digging through my life. There are certain things about me that would scandalize people if they knew." Vanessa said. "Is there anything else you want to know?"

"What's this room for?" Mel asked. "Is it yours?"

"Yes. It was empty when I acquired the premises. I later decided to repurpose it to be something of a second apartment. For when I have company. I don't like to take women back to my home, so I bring them here instead," Vanessa said casually. She seemed determined to get under Mel's skin.

And it was sure working.

"That can't be all you want to ask me, Melanie," Vanessa said.

Mel kept her mouth shut. She had a lot of questions on her mind. But there was no way she was going to ask them.

"All right then. I have a question for you." Vanessa leaned back and crossed her legs, her eyes fixed on Mel's. "Both of the times you've been in here, you haven't been able to stop staring at my riding crop."

Mel's face flushed. She'd hoped Vanessa hadn't noticed. No, that was a lie.

"Does it make you uncomfortable?" Vanessa asked.

"No," Mel said softly.

"Does it scare you?"

"No."

Vanessa examined Mel's face silently. "Could it be that you're curious?"

Mel's heart sped up. "Maybe a little…" She couldn't help herself. There was something about Vanessa that made Mel feel compelled to answer her truthfully.

"Would you like to take a closer look?" Vanessa asked, her voice a low purr. Without waiting for a response, Vanessa walked over to the bed and picked up the riding crop. She sat down on the coffee table in front of Mel and held the whip up before her chest. "It's a lovely piece of workmanship. Custom made. Leather. Narrow tip. The thinner the tip, the greater the bite." With a flick of her wrist, Vanessa slapped it against her palm.

A soft gasp escaped Mel's lips. The sound of the impact surprised her. And it set off a spark somewhere deep inside of her.

Vanessa's lips curved up almost imperceptibly. "Here." She held the whip out toward Mel, balancing it on her palms. "Hold it."

Mel turned the riding crop over in her hands. She traced the weave of the handle with her fingertips then ran them up to the supple leather tip.

"What do you think?"

"It's beautiful." Mel couldn't help but wonder what it would feel like against her skin, somewhere fleshy and tender.

"Have you ever used one?" Vanessa asked. "Or had one used on you?"

"No," Mel murmured.

"Have you ever wanted to?"

Mel hesitated. "I've thought about it. Once or twice." Another lie.

Vanessa reached out and took the crop from Mel's hands. "And when you think about it, do you see yourself as the one holding the whip? Or at the other end?"

"I don't know." The crop didn't feel at home in Mel's hands. But there was a niggling feeling at the back of her mind that prevented her from admitting the truth.

"Another way of looking at it is this," Vanessa said. "Which do you prefer? Being in control? Or giving it to someone else?" She began to tap the whip against her palm. "Being in control means having all the power. But it also means responsibility. Giving up control means you get to let go completely. But it requires you to place yourself in someone else's hands. To trust them. It can be terrifying." She stilled the crop in her hands. "And it can be exhilarating."

Mel didn't respond. The sound of her own breath seemed deafening in the silence.

"I've said before that I'm good at reading people. And I think I know the role you'd like to play. I know your type, Melanie. Ambitious. Driven. Always striving for perfection. Never allowing the slightest lapse in self-control. It must be exhausting." Vanessa ran her fingers along the shaft of the crop. "Don't you ever want to just let go of all your problems and let someone else take the reins?"

"Sometimes…" Mel had never even admitted that to herself, let alone to someone else.

"This here? This is one way to do that. To escape it all, if only for a moment. To lose yourself so completely that everything falls away and all that is left is pure ecstasy. To surrender." Vanessa leaned forward, her face barely an inch from Mel's. "Does that tempt you?"

"Yes," Mel whispered.

Vanessa brought her lips to Mel's ear. "It's more freeing than you could possibly imagine."

A shiver went through Mel's body. Vanessa's eyes seemed to strip away all her defenses. And Vanessa's face was so close to hers. Vanessa's lips were so close…

What am I thinking? Mel dropped her empty glass to the table and stood up. "I should go." Within seconds, she was out the door.

CHAPTER FOUR

*M*el sat in the lecture hall, waiting for her professor to arrive. Class didn't start for another five minutes. Leaning back in her chair, she closed her eyes and tried to clear her head of all the thoughts swirling around inside it. Inevitably, her mind went back to the same thing: Vanessa.

Since that night in Vanessa's room, Vanessa had come into The Lounge a few times while Mel was working. Mel didn't go out of her way to speak to Vanessa. But somehow their paths kept crossing. And with every word that Vanessa spoke to her, with every glance they exchanged, the pull of Mel's desire grew stronger.

Vanessa was all that Mel could think about. Vanessa's hips, swaying in her tight, silky dress. Her voice, like velvet, in Mel's ear. Her eyes, that seemed to see into the depths of Mel's being, while revealing nothing of what lay behind Vanessa's own.

And Vanessa's words. *Surrender.* It wasn't hard to figure out what she meant. Her dominant personality. The riding crop. Her talk of giving up control. It all pointed to one thing.

"Looks like you could use this."

Mel opened her eyes. Her friend Jess stood beside her, holding a coffee in each hand.

She handed one to Mel and sat down. "Finish all the readings?"

"Yep." Mel had stayed up 'til 3:00 a.m. to get them done.

"How are you always so on top of everything? I barely got halfway through them before I fell asleep." Jess groaned. "If I'm on call, I'm going to look like an idiot."

Cold calling. Those two words filled every first-year law student with dread. During class, their professors would call upon a student and ask them probing questions about the cases being discussed. Preparation was essential. Professor Carr liked to assign a few random students to be 'on call' at the start of each lecture, so no one knew if they would be on call until class started. Because law school wasn't stressful enough already.

"Here." Mel passed her notes to Jess. "I've already memorized everything."

"Thanks, Mel! What would I do without you?"

As Jess flipped through the notes, Mel closed her eyes again. Her mind picked up where it left off. She couldn't deny how the idea of submitting to another woman made her hot all over. These desires weren't new. No, they had always been there. But Mel had never allowed herself to even consider letting them play out. They went against everything she believed about herself. So she'd buried them deep inside her where they remained a half-forgotten fantasy. Until Vanessa had reawakened them.

"Mel? Hello?" Jess waved her hand in front of Mel's face.

"Huh?"

"I said, do you want to come over and study tonight? You know, for the quiz tomorrow?"

"Right. Sorry, I can't," Mel replied. "I have work."

"What's the matter with you?" Jess asked. "You've been spacing out all day. Something on your mind?"

"No, I'm fine," Mel replied.

Jess narrowed her eyes and studied Mel's face. "Or could it be... some*one*?" A smile broke out on her face. "I knew it!"

Mel sighed. Jess knew her too well. They'd been friends since freshman year of college when they ended up in most of the same pre-law classes together. Jess wanted to become a criminal defense attorney. But for now, she had to settle for interrogating her friends.

"C'mon, spill," Jess said. "I want every detail."

"There's nothing to tell," Mel said. "It's just a stupid crush. Nothing's happened."

"Do you mean, nothing's happened *yet?*"

"No. Nothing is ever going to happen."

"Why not?"

"Because I don't have the time or energy for a relationship of any kind." It wasn't a complete lie. "Why are you so interested in my love life anyway?"

Jess sighed. "Because mine is non-existent."

"What happened to Brandon?"

"You mean Brendon?"

"Yeah, him." Mel found it hard to keep up with Jess's ever-changing list of boyfriends. "I thought things were going well between you two."

Jess shrugged. "We broke up. He was kind of boring."

Mel shook her head. A week ago, Jess had been sure that Brendon was the one.

Professor Carr strode into the room. "Okay everyone, settle down."

The class fell silent. Even though Professor Carr was five foot two and old enough to be Mel's grandmother, she commanded the respect of everyone around her. She was Mel's favorite professor. She had a long and impressive career behind her. Fighting civil rights violations. Taking on corporate giants. Representing thousands in large-scale class action suits. Now she spent her days running a nation-wide legal non-profit organization. She was everything that Mel aspired to be.

"Before we get started, I have a small announcement to make," Professor Carr said. "By now, you should all be thinking about summer internships."

Murmurs went through the class. Summer internships were the first opportunity that Mel and her peers would have to get hands-on law experience, and finding an interesting internship as a first-year was almost impossible.

Professor Carr continued. "I've decided to take on a first-year student as an intern this summer. You'll be working for me personally at The Legal Services Project. For those of you who haven't heard of it, The LSP is a non-profit that provides free legal help. It connects lawyers who are willing to do pro-bono work with the clients who need it the most. And it provides individual lawyers and law firms with incentives for providing legal aid. We're making waves in the legal world. And I'm giving one of you the opportunity to be a part of it."

Mel's ears pricked up. She had to have that internship.

An opportunity to work under Professor Carr was too good to pass up. Not to mention that a number of influential people, lawyers and otherwise, were involved in the project. The connections a law student would make working there would be invaluable. So would the experience.

But Mel's interest in The LSP was far more personal. Projects like this were the reason she decided to go to law school. When she was young, her father walked out on Mel and her mother, leaving them destitute. Mel's mother spiraled into debt, depression, and alcoholism, leaving the two of them always on the verge of homelessness. It was a rough time for both of them.

It was only through legal aid services that Mel's mother was able to pursue her ex-husband for child support and get her debt under control. The lawyer assigned to her mother was a kindly old woman who did far more than her job required to help them get their lives back on track. Mel would never forget how much of a difference the woman had made in her life. She wanted to do the same for others someday.

"I know that a lot of you will be interested," Professor Carr said. "So I'm going to make my choice based on merit. And I don't mean whoever gets the highest grades. Out in the real world, it doesn't matter what grade you got on your final. To make it as a lawyer, you need to be willing to put in the hard work. You need to have a deep understanding of the law. You need to be able to use that knowledge as a weapon. So if you want this internship, show me that you have what it takes. Come to class prepared. Pay attention to my lectures. Prove that your understanding of the law goes beyond what's written in your textbooks. Impress me, and the internship is yours."

The class broke out into loud whispers. Mel wasn't the only one excited about the internship. She would have some tough competition.

"Settle down, everyone. Let's get started." As the conversation faded, Professor Carr put on her glasses and picked up a sheet of paper. "The students on call today are-"

The class collectively held its breath as Professor Carr rattled off a list of names.

"-and Melanie Greene."

Mel downed the rest of her coffee in one gulp. She was prepared. She had this.

Mel made it through the hour without any problems. Not everyone was that lucky. One of her classmates had slowly broken down over the course of the lecture. She was almost in tears by the end of the class. Most law students, especially those at her prestigious school, were highly competitive. Many of them didn't handle failure well.

"That internship," Jess said. "You're going to go for it, right?"

"Definitely." Mel gathered her things, and they joined the stream of students heading out of the lecture hall. "How about you?"

"No way. I'm not crazy enough to want to compete with you and all the others who want it. Besides, I already have an internship in mind. I'll be spending my summer at the District Attorney's office."

"Melanie," Professor Carr called out. "A moment, please."

Mel told Jess she'd catch up with her later and walked over to the professor's desk.

"You did well today," Professor Carr said. "Handled my questions like a pro."

"It was an interesting case. I did lots of research."

"I expected nothing less. So, about The LSP internship. Are you interested?"

"Definitely! Working at a place like that would be a dream come true."

"I'm not going to lie. I'm rooting for you, Mel. The others? They only want the internship because it will look good on their resumes. But I know that you care about this kind of project. I was the one who reviewed your law school application. And your personal statement showed that you're doing this for all the right reasons."

Mel shifted from one foot to the other. Her personal statement had touched upon her experience with that lawyer who had helped her mother, and how it had affected her life. Of course, she didn't mention the parts of her child-hood that had really shaped her. Those weren't the kind of things she could put in a law school entry essay. But her essay had revealed more of herself than she usually gave to people, even those closest to her.

"You're a talented student, Melanie. I want to see you succeed." Professor Carr crossed her arms. "But I'm not going to hand you that internship. It wouldn't be fair to anyone, you included. Earn it. Don't disappoint me."

Mel nodded.

"I'll let you go now."

"Thanks, Professor Carr." As Mel left the lecture hall, she

knew it was time to put Vanessa out of her mind. There was no time for games, not now. She had to stay focused.

"Coming to drinks tonight, Mel?" James asked.

Mel gave him an apologetic smile. "Sorry, James, I have a quiz tomorrow. I'll be up all night studying."

"You're off the hook this time. But one of these days, I'll get through to you." James wandered off back to the bar.

Mel shook her head. It was an hour into her shift and the night was beginning to ramp up. There would be no chatting behind the bar tonight. She went over to a recently vacated table and began to clean up. As Mel placed a half-finished bottle of very expensive wine on her tray, something caught her eye. Someone.

Vanessa. The crowd seemed to part before her as she walked through it with long, purposeful strides and a regal air. She looked more stunning than ever. She wore a blue silk cocktail dress that flowed down her hips like water. Her long dark hair hung loose around her shoulders. Her pearlescent skin seemed to shimmer under the sparkling lights.

Vanessa strode closer. She wasn't heading for her usual seat. She was heading for the corridor that lead to her room upstairs. And it was right behind Mel. Mel stood frozen in place, unable to tear her eyes off the woman who had taken over her thoughts since that night.

As Vanessa passed Mel, she said nothing, but simply shot Mel a look. The same look she had given Mel in her room that night. The look that made Mel want to come apart.

Vanessa slipped around the corner. Mel inched toward the corridor, as if drawn by a magnet, and peered around the corner. The door at the bottom of the stairs was ajar, a thin beam of light shining through the tiny crack. Mel crept closer, pulled the door open, and looked up the stairs.

Before Mel knew what she was doing, she followed Vanessa up to her room and knocked on the door.

CHAPTER FIVE

"**C**ome in," Vanessa called from inside the room.

Mel opened the door. In the dim light, she could make out Vanessa's figure reclining in an armchair. Something long and thin lay across her lap. The riding crop.

Mel had stumbled right into Vanessa's trap.

Vanessa stood up, whip in hand, and walked toward Mel. She reached around Mel's body and closed the door. It clicked shut, locking them in. The music from downstairs faded to a soft hum.

"Why did you follow me in here, Melanie?" Vanessa asked.

"I want to know," Mel said, her voice barely a whisper. "I want to know what you meant about giving up control. Surrender."

Vanessa pressed the tip of the crop into the base of Mel's neck and drew it down the center of her chest. "You know exactly what I mean."

Mel's lips parted slightly. Vanessa was so close that she

could feel the heat radiating from Vanessa's skin and Vanessa's breath on her neck.

"We both know what you want. We both know what you're longing for. I can give it to you." Vanessa took Mel's chin in her hands and tilted Mel's face up toward her. "All you have to do is let go."

Mel's heart pounded. She stared back at Vanessa, her mind swimming in conflict and doubt. Then she closed her eyes and let her body take over. At once, Vanessa's lips were on hers, a soft, light kiss that lingered even after they parted.

Mel exhaled slowly. She didn't know who had kissed the other first. All she knew was that it had charged the room with an energy that desperately needed to be dispelled.

Vanessa dropped the riding crop to the floor with a clatter. She grabbed Mel's wrists, pinning them above her head, and kissed her again. This time the kiss was deep, hungry, insistent. Mel responded in kind.

Vanessa pressed her body against Mel's, trapping Mel against the wall with her hips. "I can tell how much you want me." Vanessa pushed her thigh firmly between Mel's legs, stoking the fire deep inside her. "I've wanted you since the first night I saw you in my club. And I always get what I want."

Her words sent a ripple of heat through Mel's body. Vanessa released Mel's wrists and began to tear at her clothes. She ripped Mel's blouse from the waistband of her skirt and up over her head, then unclasped Mel's bra and pulled it from her shoulders. She swept her hands up Mel's chest, teasing her pebbled nipples with her fingertips.

Everything was happening so fast. One moment, Vanessa's hands were grasping at Mel's breasts. The next, they were down at the hem of her skirt, pushing it up around her waist. Then Vanessa's fingers were between Mel's thighs, pressing her wet panties into her lips.

A silent moan formed in Mel's mouth. Vanessa trailed her lips down Mel's neck, all the way to her chest, and took Mel's nipple into her mouth, sucking, licking, and flicking.

Mel gasped and writhed against the wall. Vanessa's skin. Vanessa's mouth. Vanessa's sweet, floral scent. Every part of her was intoxicating.

Vanessa slipped her hand inside Mel's panties and ran a finger up and down her folds. Mel's head rolled back, and she grabbed the wall behind her to steady herself as darts of pleasure shot through her. Vanessa's fingers and lips seemed to zero in on places where Mel had never been touched before.

Vanessa slid her finger further down and drew slow, teasing circles. "Do you want me? Do you want me inside you?"

"Yes," Mel said between breaths.

"I want to hear you say it. I want to hear you beg."

"Please, Vanessa… I want you so badly!" Mel meant every word she said. "I need you inside of me. Please!"

Satisfied, Vanessa slid a finger inside her, then another. Mel let out a strangled sigh as Vanessa found that sensitive spot inside her. Her thumb worked its way up to Mel's stiff bud, rubbing against it with every thrust of her fingers.

Wedged between Vanessa's body and the wall, Mel could do little more than cling to the other woman, her hands slipping on the smooth silk of Vanessa's dress. It didn't take long before Mel felt control slipping away.

"Come for me," Vanessa said. "I want to hear you scream."

It was as if Mel's body had been waiting for Vanessa's permission. She came hard and fast, a wordless cry on her lips.

Mel leaned against the wall behind her, her arms still around Vanessa's shoulders. Vanessa's satin dress was cool against her skin.

Vanessa brought her hand up to Mel's face, drew Mel's bottom lip down, and gently pushed her fingers into the other woman's mouth. Mel sucked on them lazily. She could taste herself on Vanessa's skin.

"So eager," Vanessa said. "So obedient. Do you like following my orders? Do you like pleasing me?"

"Yes," Mel said softly.

"Then show me."

Vanessa spun them both around until her back was against the wall. Mel's breath caught in her chest. She desperately wanted to touch Vanessa, to taste her. Instead, she stood and waited, gazing up at Vanessa with a silent plea in her eyes.

Vanessa answered it with a single word. "Kneel."

Mel's knees crumbled beneath her.

A faint smile crossed Vanessa's lips. "Go on."

Mel slid her hands up the sides of Vanessa's legs and under her dress until her fingers reached the soft black lace of Vanessa's panties. She drew them down Vanessa's hips, all the way to the floor, and pushed her slippery silk dress up to her stomach. Vanessa's scent was dizzying. Anchoring herself on Vanessa's hips, she traced her tongue up the soft skin of Vanessa's inner thighs. Vanessa was as wet as Mel had been, and Mel had barely even touched her.

Mel kissed the peak where Vanessa's lips met, then slid her tongue between them. She ran it up and down in long, languid strokes, savoring Vanessa's taste. Mel probed with the tip of her tongue until she found Vanessa's tiny, hidden peak. She stroked and sucked it thirstily.

"Don't stop." Vanessa threaded her fingers through Mel's hair and pulled Mel harder into her, bucking and rolling her hips against Mel's mouth.

Mel redoubled her efforts, relishing the satisfaction she was giving Vanessa. Vanessa didn't make a single sound, but Mel could feel Vanessa's thighs quiver around her. Mel ignored the ache in her knees from the hard floor.

Vanessa gripped tighter at Mel's hair and her movements became more and more frantic. At last, Vanessa's entire body shuddered, and her mouth opened in silent ecstasy. Mel lapped away, drawing every last drop of pleasure out of her. When Vanessa's body stilled, Mel released her hips and let her silky dress slide back down her legs.

Vanessa let out a deep breath. She reached down toward Mel and cupped Mel's face in her hands, drawing her up onto her feet. Vanessa tucked a stray lock of Mel's hair behind her ear and whispered into it. "I believe you have a shift to finish."

Instantly, the spell was broken. Mel cursed. How long had she been in here? Their frenzied encounter had both felt like it had stretched out into eternity and had been over in a heartbeat.

Mel gathered her clothes and began to pull them on. The

club would be getting busy now. Had James and the others noticed Mel's absence?

"Here." Vanessa handed Mel's skirt to her, a hint of amusement in her eyes.

Mel finished dressing, then smoothed down her hair in a nearby mirror. As she turned to leave, Vanessa pulled Mel back to her in a ravenous kiss. Mel had to tear her body away when she felt herself sinking into Vanessa again.

Mel dashed from the room. She stopped at the bottom of the stairs to catch her breath.

What the hell just happened?

CHAPTER SIX

*A*nother night at The Lounge. Another night, and no sign of Vanessa. Their late-night tryst in Vanessa's room had left Mel more confused than ever. She had no idea what it meant. Was it a one-time moment of passion? Or the start of something more? Did Vanessa even want to see her again? Mel had no way to contact her. All she could do was wait for Vanessa to turn up again.

Mel sighed. This all seemed so unreal. Mel didn't normally have sex with women she barely knew, let alone women like Vanessa. She was far too disciplined to allow herself to be controlled by lust. Yet she couldn't stop thinking about how Vanessa's lips made her melt, or how Vanessa's touch made her quiver. How when Vanessa had ordered Mel to get on her knees, her body had obeyed before her conscious mind even registered the command. This simple act of submission had felt completely natural to her. But there was still a part of her that resisted it all.

"Everything okay?" James asked. "You look distracted."

"Just thinking about school," Mel lied.

"I should have guessed. So, Mel, how confident are you working behind the bar? Ben had to leave early and I need someone to take his place."

"Sure, I can do it."

"Great. I'll be in the back. Come find me if you have any problems. It's pretty quiet tonight. I'm sure you'll be fine."

Mel nodded and slid behind the bar. Soon, she had a steady flow of customers. She had no trouble keeping up. James had taught her well. Eventually, she got into a rhythm, working on muscle memory alone, allowing her thoughts to wander. How well did James know Vanessa? Mel wanted to ask him about her. Would it be suspicious if she did?

The stream of customers gradually died down. Mel took the time to tidy up the bar. She was returning a few bottles of tequila to their place on the shelf behind her when she heard a familiar voice.

"Hello, Melanie."

Mel turned. "Vanessa?"

Vanessa stood before her in a sleek red dress. A thin gold necklace with a sapphire pendant hung around her neck. Mel's eyes fell to Vanessa's lips. They were the same deep red color as her dress. Mel couldn't help but recall how those lips had felt on her lips. And on her nipples. And for a brief moment, she imagined how they would feel on certain other parts of her body.

"Make me a drink," Vanessa said. "Your choice."

"Sure." Mel chose one of the club's signature cocktails, a variation of a whiskey sour. She could practically make it with her eyes closed now. She placed it before Vanessa on the bar.

Vanessa sampled the drink. "Not bad."

Mel couldn't contain herself any longer. "I've been waiting for you to come back."

"Have you?" Vanessa leaned down on the bar. "Why?"

"Because the other night was incredible. Because falling to my knees before you made me feel freer than I've felt in years. Because it made me realize that there's this whole side of me that craves this…" Mel trailed off, suddenly self-conscious.

"What exactly is it that you crave, Melanie?" Vanessa asked. "I want to hear it from you."

Mel looked straight into Vanessa's eyes. "Submission."

Vanessa beckoned Mel closer. "If you let me, I can show you what it really means to submit. I can make your darkest desires reality. I can grant you your wildest fantasies. Do you want that?" She slid her hand up Mel's arm.

"Yes." Vanessa's touch sent a shiver along Mel's skin. "More than anything."

The door to the back room swung open and James emerged. Mel snapped back upright. Vanessa seemed unfazed.

"Vanessa." James's voice was subdued. "Do you have a minute?"

Vanessa nodded. She took another sip of her drink and pushed it toward Mel. "Hold on to this for me. Our conversation isn't over."

James looked from Vanessa to Mel and back again, scratching his beard. Mel busied herself behind the bar, hoping that her expression hadn't given anything away.

Vanessa and James walked off to the side. Mel focused her attention on cleaning up the bar. But her curiosity won out. Vanessa and James were too far away for Mel to hear them. Instead, she watched the conversation out of the corner of her eye. She couldn't tell what they were talking about. After a while, James placed a hand on Vanessa's arm and spoke into her ear.

Vanessa transformed in an instant. Her expression darkened and her body tensed. Then the two of them started arguing. Vanessa was clearly angry about something, although her anger didn't seem to be directed at James. As the conversation died down, James placed a hand on Vanessa's shoulder as if to try to calm her. Mel was surprised by the intimateness of the gesture. She didn't know that they were that close. Before Mel could finish her thought, Vanessa turned and stormed off toward the corridor that led to her room.

What was that about?

James returned to the bar, his face scrunched up with concern.

"Is everything okay?" Mel asked.

"Yep. Just business stuff." He looked at Mel curiously. "What were you and Vanessa talking about before I interrupted you?"

"She was just saying hi," Mel said quickly.

"Right."

Mel couldn't tell if James was convinced or not. She took Vanessa's drink and placed it behind the bar. As the night went on, the drink sat there, the ice slowly melting. By the time Mel's shift ended, Vanessa hadn't emerged from her room. Mel wasn't bothered by the fact that Vanessa hadn't returned to finish their conversation. It was clear that Vanessa had more important things on her mind.

Mel made her way home. As she walked through her apartment door, her phone buzzed. It was a text message from an unknown number. As soon as Mel read the message, she knew who it was from. It contained no greeting, no explanation. Just a single sentence.

I'll be in touch.

Mel sat at her table, her laptop open in front of her, half a dozen textbooks stacked up beside it. Her eyes glazed over as she scanned the screen. She took off her headphones in defeat. She should have gone to the library instead of staying in. It was hard to get anything done in her tiny apartment.

She would take a small break and then get back to it. Mel had to work much harder than her classmates to stay on top of everything. Most of them didn't have to work while they were at law school. They were trust fund kids, or at the very least had parents who helped support them. But Mel didn't have that luxury.

And for Mel, simply doing well enough to pass wasn't an option. If she wanted a good job when she graduated, she had to maintain a competitive GPA. She had to remain disciplined. It was what got her this far, and it was the only way she knew how to be.

Ever since Mel was a kid, she'd had no one else in her life to provide her with structure and direction. Her father had left when Mel was young, and her alcoholic mother had never been a reliable parent. She resented Mel for being a constant reminder of the man who had broken her heart and left her with nothing. So she did the bare minimum, keeping Mel fed, clothed, and sheltered from the cold. But otherwise, Mel was on her own.

So Mel took control of her life, to the point where it became an obsession. Eventually, she decided to focus all her energy on making a better life for herself. College was her ticket out of her hometown, and she'd thrown everything into her studies to escape.

Mel stretched out her arms and looked around the room. Her hard work had paid off. She'd left her old life far behind her. But after years and years of fighting her way through the world, she wanted to just give in to temptation and let go of it all.

Mel shut her laptop. She needed to go for a run.

There was a knock on her door. Mel jumped. No one ever came to her apartment unannounced, and she wasn't expecting a delivery.

Mel opened the door. A woman stood before her, dressed in a crisp black suit and a matching overcoat. Her short, dark hair was parted at the side, and her shoes were immaculate. She looked to be around forty. Did she have the wrong apartment number? Or was she lost?

"Melanie?" the woman asked. She had a thick accent that Mel couldn't place.

Mel nodded.

The woman pulled a package out from under her arm. It was a black box with a silk ribbon tied around it. "A gift for you. From Ms. Harper."

"Ms. Harper?"

"Yes. Ms. Vanessa Harper."

"Oh." Mel took the package from the woman. "Thanks."

With a nod, the woman walked off down the hall.

Mel shut the door, her head filled with questions. Vanessa was sending her gifts? And having them hand-delivered to her apartment? She placed the package on the table, eyeing it warily. Mel had always felt uncomfortable receiving gifts. Her mother always saw them as 'charity.' She'd said that if Mel accepted handouts, people would think they were poor. If only she'd cared as much about Mel as she cared about what other people thought of her.

Mel's phone buzzed. It was a message from the same unknown number as the other night after her shift. Mel hadn't saved the number, but the digits were imprinted on her mind. She opened the text.

Tomorrow. 9 pm. Same place. Wear my gift.

Wear her gift? Immediately, Mel's reservations about the package were replaced by excitement. She grabbed the box from the table and untied the ribbon. She lifted the lid and was met with layer after layer of black tissue paper, until finally, Mel reached her prize. It was a set of lacy lingerie in a shade of purple so deep that it was almost black. She held the bra up to the light. The thin, delicate lace was almost entirely transparent. There was a clasp at the front between the two cups. The panties were made of the same sheer fabric, and tied up at the sides with little bows. Both pieces left little to the imagination.

Mel ran her fingers over the soft lace. She had never owned anything so luxurious. How much did this cost?

It didn't matter. If Vanessa wanted to Mel to come to her dressed in pretty things, who was Mel to deny her?

Mel put the bra and panties back in the box and threw herself down onto the bed. She read the text again carefully. She had no idea what Vanessa was planning. But she knew that if she went to Vanessa's room tomorrow night, there would be no going back.

CHAPTER SEVEN

*M*el walked into The Lounge the next night with Vanessa's gift on under her clothes. She gave the bar a narrow berth, hoping to slip by unnoticed by her coworkers, and made her way up to Vanessa's room. The door at the top of the stairs loomed before her. She took a deep breath and knocked.

"Come in, Melanie."

Mel stepped into the room and shut the door behind her. Vanessa sat in her armchair, a glass of whiskey in her hand. Her raven hair was gathered over one shoulder, and she wore a black satin robe, belted at the waist. Mel couldn't help but wonder if she was wearing anything underneath it.

"Come here," Vanessa said.

Mel walked over and stood before her.

"Are you wearing my gift?"

"Yes, Vanessa."

"Show me."

Mel slid off her coat and let it fall to the floor. She did the same with her dress, leaving her standing before

Vanessa in nothing but the lingerie gifted to her by the other woman. Vanessa stood up and walked around Mel in a slow circle, inspecting her slight figure from every angle. Under Vanessa's unwavering gaze, Mel felt even more naked than she was.

"You look divine," Vanessa said.

Mel's breath quickened. The hungry look on Vanessa's face made Mel feel like her prey.

"If I'm going to give you what you crave, you will have to give me something in return," Vanessa said. "Complete and utter surrender. You will submit to me. You will obey me. You will belong to me in every sense of the word. Do you understand?"

"Yes, Vanessa."

A slight smile played on Vanessa's lips. "You're going to need a safe word. Do you know what that is?"

Mel nodded.

"What will yours be?"

Mel closed her eyes and searched her mind. "Velvet," she said. Like Vanessa's smooth, low voice.

"Velvet it is." Vanessa sat back on the arm of the chair. "Go sit on the bed."

Mel walked over to the bed. Up close, she saw that each of the four bedposts had a black silk scarf tied to it. Anticipation and anxiety warred in Mel's mind. She sat down. The mattress was firm and springy.

"There's a blindfold on the pillow next to you," Vanessa continued. "Put it on and lie down."

Mel picked up the blindfold and tied it around her eyes. Darkness flooded her vision. She lay down on the bed and rested her head on the pillow. The silky bedsheets felt cool against her skin. Vanessa's bare feet padded against the floorboards as she approached Mel on the bed.

"Raise your arms up to the corners of the bed." With a practiced hand, Vanessa secured Mel's wrists to the bedposts, then repeated the process on her ankles.

Mel's heart pounded. She lay spread-eagled on the bed in nothing but the sheerest of lingerie. She tugged at her bonds to test their strength. In the same moment, Mel realized that she could no longer hear or feel Vanessa's presence. "Vanessa?"

"I'm right here." Vanessa's voice came from somewhere beside Mel. She traced her fingers along Mel's stomach all the way up to her cheek. "Stop thinking. Stop worrying. Just feel." Vanessa kissed her gently.

Mel cleared her mind and relaxed her body. She stopped straining to hear, and feel, and see. She surrendered to the darkness and focused her mind on what she could sense. The hammering of her heart, the whoosh of her breath. The scent of Vanessa's perfume, jasmine and rose. The touch of Vanessa's fingertips on her skin. It was like she and Vanessa were the only two people in the world.

The bed swayed underneath Mel as Vanessa climbed onto it. Her long, silky hair brushed against Mel's skin. Vanessa ran her hands over Mel's body, touching every inch of her skin. Silence hung in the air. Mel didn't dare speak, fearing that a single word would break the spell.

Vanessa slid her hands up to the clasp at the front of Mel's bra. With one deft motion, it was undone. Mel's breasts spilled out of the cups as it fell away. Vanessa caressed them with her hands, her fingertips sweeping over Mel's nipples.

"How does it feel to be at my mercy?" Vanessa asked.

"Good. So good..." A ripple of delight went through Mel's body. With her senses dampened, Vanessa's touch was electric.

Vanessa shifted down the bed and straddled Mel. Her weight was heavy on Mel's small, bound frame. As Vanessa's body pressed against hers, she realized that Vanessa was naked. She yearned to break free and tear off the blindfold, and touch and kiss Vanessa's soft skin. But bound as she was, she could do nothing but lay there. Bound as she was, she was powerless to stop Vanessa. But stopping Vanessa was the last thing she wanted.

Vanessa drew a line of kisses down Mel's stomach. Mel trembled. Slowly and gingerly, Vanessa untied the ribbons at the sides of Mel's panties. Mel lifted her hips as Vanessa pulled them out from under her. She felt like a gift that Vanessa was unwrapping. Vanessa slid her hands all the way up the insides of Mel's legs and dipped her head between Mel's thighs. Vanessa's hot breath on Mel's mound sent a wave of warmth through her. Vanessa kissed the soft, sensitive skin of Mel's inner thighs. Her kisses turned into nibbles, then gentle bites. Mel groaned and arched herself up toward Vanessa.

"So impatient," Vanessa said. "You're not trying to take charge, are you?"

Mel bit her lip. "No, Vanessa."

"The only sounds I want to hear from you are cries of pleasure."

Vanessa dragged her fingernails down Mel's sides and grabbed the other woman's ass cheeks, pulling Mel harder into her. Finally, she slid her tongue between Mel's lips and drew it up Mel's folds, eliciting soft gasps.

Mel twitched on the bed as Vanessa devoured her. Every sweep of Vanessa's tongue, every brush of her lips sent a tremor through Mel's body and murmurs spilling from her mouth. Vanessa had complete control over Mel's pleasure, and she was determined to show it. Vanessa teased and toyed with Mel until she was close to peaking, then she held Mel there, at the precipice, never quite letting her tip over the edge.

Mel twisted and tugged, fighting her restraints. She wanted to scream. She wanted to plead with Vanessa for release. But she understood the rules of this game. She had to take whatever Vanessa gave her with nothing less than gratitude. And eventually, her submission would be rewarded.

Once again, Vanessa brought Mel to the edge. But this time, she kept going. Mel let out a cry, bucking and thrashing as her orgasm rolled through her. Vanessa's mouth was unrelenting, licking and sucking away until Mel fell back down to the bed and her body calmed.

Vanessa kissed Mel, stealing the last of her breath. She could taste herself on the other woman's lips. Vanessa pulled the blindfold from Mel's eyes and untied her wrists and ankles. Mel blinked rapidly, her eyes readjusting to the light.

Vanessa lay down on her side next to Mel. As Mel recovered, she ran her eyes up Vanessa's body, drinking her in. This was the first time she had seen Vanessa naked. Her curves seemed more pronounced, and her dark hair, both on her head and the small patch between her legs, stood out against her milky skin. Her areolas were a rosy pink on her pale breasts.

Vanessa watched Mel watch her. For whatever reason, it made Mel blush. Vanessa smiled and pulled Mel into an embrace. After being restrained, her senses muffled, having Vanessa's arms around her felt heavenly.

"Did you mean what you said earlier? About belonging to me?" Vanessa asked.

"Yes, Vanessa."

"Then we'll have to talk about exactly what that means. But it can wait."

They lay in silence. As Mel came down from her post-orgasm daze, familiar doubts crept into her thoughts.

"What's the matter?" Vanessa asked.

"It's nothing," Mel mumbled.

"Tell me." Vanessa's usually inscrutable face wore a look of concern.

Mel's resolve wavered, and she finally gave voice to the thing that had been bothering her since the first time she walked into Vanessa's room. "It's just that, I want this. I want to explore this side of me so much that it makes me ache. But I'm not a submissive person. I'm not passive, or helpless. But I can't help but wonder. Does this mean I'm weak? For wanting to be submissive? For wanting an escape?"

"No, Melanie. You're not weak at all."

"Then why do I want this? Why do I crave this?"

"Being submissive in bed has nothing to do with who you are out in the world. And submission does not equal weakness. In fact, it takes a great deal of strength to do this."

"It doesn't feel like it takes strength. It's easy for me. Effortless."

"I'm sure it is. But it takes strength to embrace that side of you. And to act on it. I've tried it myself, you know. Only a few times. I wanted to get a better understanding of what it feels like to be on the other side. It was terrifying. I could never do it again."

Mel was surprised. She couldn't imagine Vanessa being subservient or vulnerable. She always seemed so fearless. Who was Vanessa behind her impenetrably cool façade?

"It does take strength to do this, Melanie. Putting yourself in someone else's hands. Making yourself vulnerable to them. Trusting them with your everything. You are anything but weak." Vanessa kissed Mel gently on the lips. "And you should never, ever be ashamed of your desires."

"Yes, Vanessa." Mel snuggled in closer to her.

"Now, about these desires of yours." Vanessa reached out and ran her hands along Mel's side, following the contours of her body. "I want to know more. All your secret fantasies? I want to hear about them. Tell me everything."

CHAPTER EIGHT

*M*el sat in class, eyelids drooping at her professor's low monotone. She looked over at Jess. Her friend was having a hard time paying attention too. She was doodling in the margin of her notebook, a vacant look in her eyes.

Mel's bag vibrated on the floor beneath her. Trying to be discreet, she pulled her phone out and peeked at the screen. She grinned.

"A message from your lover?" Jess asked.

A student sitting in front of them turned to glare at them. Mel shushed Jess.

"Is that a yes?" Jess asked, quieter this time.

"Maybe." Mel unlocked her phone and read the message.

What time do you get out of class? V.

5 pm, Mel sent. She thought for a moment and typed. *Why?* Her finger hovered over the send button. She erased the message.

"So are you going to tell me who she is?" Jess asked.

"Just someone from work."

"A coworker?"

Mel hesitated. "She's a customer." It wasn't a lie. Although she trusted Jess, Mel didn't feel right giving away Vanessa's 'secret.'

"Wow. Isn't everyone who goes there a millionaire?" Jess asked. "I'm totally jealous. What's it like dating someone like that?"

"We're not dating." At least, Mel didn't think they were.

"Then what is it? Are you her sugar baby?"

"Definitely not. It's purely physical." Mel fiddled with her pen. "I doubt she's interested in anything more."

"Why not?"

By now they had both given up on the lecture. Luckily, their eighty-year-old professor had poor hearing.

"I can't imagine someone like Vanessa being interested in someone like me," Mel said. "She's from a completely different world than me. She drinks whiskey that costs more than my month's rent. And she's so successful, and sophisticated, and elegant."

"All of those things are superficial, Mel. Do you think she cares you don't have money? When it comes to love, none of that stuff matters."

"Love? Love isn't even a possibility. I'm not interested in her that way. I'm not even looking for a relationship."

"Come on, Mel. It's been ages since everything with Kim. Are you going to spend the rest of your life alone because of one bad relationship?"

'Bad' was an understatement. Mel sighed. "I don't know. It doesn't matter. I don't need any distractions right now."

"You can't shut everyone out forever, Mel. Life is so much better when you have people to share it with."

Mel shrugged. "I have plenty of people in my life. And I like my life the way it is."

"If you say so." Jess stretched out in her chair. "So, her name is Vanessa?"

"Yeah."

"What's she like?"

"She's amazing. Gorgeous. A little older. And she's so confident and magnetic. She turns heads when she walks into a room."

"Look at you, all dreamy-eyed. The sex must be something else if she's making you act like this."

Mel rolled her eyes. She looked down at her phone. Still nothing from Vanessa. Jess was right. She was obsessing. Even though Mel definitely didn't have feelings for Vanessa, she would have to keep her guard up. The temptation was there.

Five o'clock rolled around and Mel and Jess made their way across campus.

"Finally," Jess said. "I thought this day would never end."

"Me too. I can't wait to go home and go for a run."

"Seriously? That's what you want to do at the end of a long day? I will never understand you."

They reached the main entrance. As they walked past the parking lot, Mel froze on the spot. "Vanessa?"

Vanessa stood in the parking lot leaning against the side of a sleek, black convertible. The top was down, showing off the white leather interior.

Vanessa took off her sunglasses and gave Mel a brief wave.

Jess's eyes widened. "Is that her? Vanessa?"

Mel nodded. Her mind went back to high school when

girls would get picked up by their older boyfriends in banged up wrecks that to their teenage eyes were luxury cars. Of course, Mel was never one of those girls. She'd known she was gay since she was five, and dating girls was not an option at her conservative high school.

"Wow, she's gorgeous." Jess stared at Vanessa, wide-eyed. "If I was into women, I'd be all over her too."

Mel had to agree that Vanessa looked stunning. She was dressed a long tan coat that went down to her knees, and glossy black heels. Her dark, wavy hair was blowing in the wind, and she wore her signature red lipstick.

"Sorry, Jess, I gotta go. See you tomorrow." Mel hurried over to Vanessa, leaving Jess to gawk from the sidewalk. Mel was torn between shrinking with embarrassment and running up to Vanessa and throwing her arms around her.

"Hello, Melanie." Vanessa pulled Mel into an embrace and kissed her on the cheek.

"What are you doing here?"

"What do you think? Picking you up."

Mel looked over her shoulder. There were a handful of students standing around waiting for rides. And they were all looking Mel's way. Expensive sports cars weren't uncommon at Mel's prestigious school, but women like Vanessa were rare everywhere.

"Where are we going?" Mel asked.

"I thought I'd take you somewhere nice so we can talk." Vanessa opened the passenger side door. "Hop in."

Mel got into the car and buckled her seatbelt. She looked around. The interior was as luxurious as the outside of the car.

"Do you like it?" Vanessa got into the driver's seat.

"It's nice. But I don't know much about cars."

"My father was a mechanic," Vanessa said. "He was always working on something in the garage. As soon as I was old enough to hold a wrench, I was his little helper." Vanessa saw the look of surprise on Mel's face. "What, did you think I was born with a silver spoon in my mouth?"

"I hadn't really thought about it…" Mel found it hard to see the elegant, glamorous Vanessa as anything other than who she was now.

"I wasn't born into this life. I grew up as an only child in a normal working-class family. I had to fight to get to where I am. Everything I have, I've earned through hard work." Vanessa put her sunglasses on and turned the key in the ignition. The engine burst into life. "I've missed this sound. I don't often get the chance to take my Maserati for a spin. It's far more exciting than being chauffeured around everywhere."

As soon as they left the parking lot, Vanessa slammed her heeled foot on the pedal, sending them flying down the road. Mel clutched the side of the seat as the wind whipped around them.

Vanessa glanced at Mel, a hint of amusement on her face. "You should see what it's like on the track. It's the most incredible feeling. It's almost like flying."

As they sped off from a red light, Mel began to relax. Although the sheer power and acceleration made Mel feel like she was on a roller coaster, Vanessa wasn't driving recklessly. She was in complete control the entire time.

Still, Mel was relieved when Vanessa parked the car and announced that they had arrived.

A few minutes and an elevator ride later, Mel and Vanessa walked onto the roof of a small cocktail bar. There were only a handful of other people around. They took their seats at a long bar that ran around the edges of the rooftop. The glass walls allowed for a view of the city below.

"Wow." Mel leaned forward and looked through the glass. The sun was setting, and the sky was a haze of orange, pink, and blue.

"This is one of my favorite spots in the entire city," Vanessa said. "Especially at this time of the evening. I love catching that moment when the sun disappears behind the skyscrapers and the city comes alive with light. It's spectacular."

A waiter brought out their drinks. Whiskey for Vanessa, and a cocktail recommended by the bartender for Mel. They chatted about nothing of consequence as they watched the sun sink below the horizon.

"So, Melanie." Vanessa ran her fingers through her hair. Not a curl was out of place, despite the windy drive. "It's time we had a little talk."

"What do you want to talk about?" Mel asked.

"About this. About what we're doing."

Mel pushed the ice around her drink with a straw, recalling the conversation she'd had with Jess earlier. Did Vanessa want their physical affair to be something more?

"I'm making you nervous?" Vanessa said. "Why?"

"I have been wondering. What exactly is it that you want? It's just, I'm not looking for anything serious. Like a relationship. Not right now."

Vanessa raised an eyebrow. "Last time we got together, I tied you to a bed. Do you really think I'm interested in romance?"

Relief flooded Mel's body. "I guess not."

"I assure you, I'm not looking for a relationship either. Well, not in the conventional sense. I want nothing more than what I've already told you. I want to show you all about the pleasures of submission. Do you still want that?"

"Yes. I do."

"Are you sure? No more reservations?"

"I'm sure." That voice at the back of Mel's head telling her that her submissive desires made her weak? It had faded to nothing after that conversation with Vanessa.

"That's what I want to talk about. It's very clear from what you've told me that you want more than being tied to a bed. Am I right?"

"Yes." Mel flushed. She had been far more open with Vanessa that night than she had intended. Vanessa seemed to have that effect on her.

"If we're going to do this, there are quite a few things we need to discuss," Vanessa said. "We need to be responsible. I'm not going to just tie you up and flog you without any prior discussion."

Vanessa's words planted a very sexy image in Mel's mind. She couldn't help but grin.

"Really, Melanie?" Vanessa shook her head with a smile. "You just can't help yourself, can you?"

Mel shrugged sheepishly. She found it hard enough to keep her imagination in check even without Vanessa feeding it suggestions.

"In all seriousness, you need to know what we're getting

into. BDSM can be risky. Physically, mentally, emotionally. So it's essential that we communicate. About boundaries, consent, limits, and a whole host of other things. You already have a safe word. That's a start. But do you know what your hard limits are? The things that you won't do under any circumstances?"

"I haven't really thought about it," Mel said. "But there are definitely things I never want to try."

"You don't have to tell me them now. I'll give you some time to think about everything. And this is an ongoing conversation, not a one-time discussion. But what I need you to understand is that this kind of relationship is all about communication."

"Okay." Mel tried to ignore Vanessa's use of the word 'relationship.'

Vanessa's phone rang. "I should check this. It could be work." She took her phone out of her bag and looked at it, an almost imperceptible frown on her face.

"Is everything okay?" Mel asked.

"Yes. It's nothing important." Vanessa silenced the phone and slid it back into her bag. "Now, where were we? Is there anything you'd like to ask me?"

Mel thought for a moment. "What do you get out of this? Out of having someone submit to you?"

Vanessa looked out through the glass. "I've said it before. We're alike, you and I. Hard working, ambitious, obsessed with control and self-discipline. It can be consuming. We both want a temporary escape from all of that. It simply manifests in us in different ways." Vanessa looked back at Mel. "You want to give up control, to lose yourself in a way that you would never allow yourself to out in the real world. Me? I want control in its purest, most absolute form. What I do gives me complete power over another person in the most intimate of ways. I become her Master, her whole world. Her everything."

Mel felt a chill wash over her.

"There's an immense satisfaction that comes from having the power to make someone fall apart with nothing more than a word. Or, a touch." Without breaking her gaze, Vanessa placed her hand on Mel's knee under the bar and slid it up the inside of Mel's thigh.

Mel's body stiffened as Vanessa's hand crept higher. Mel looked around. Could anyone see them?

"All those fantasies you told me about? I'm going to grant them, and so much more. I'll show you how good it feels to relinquish control. I'll take you to heights of pleasure that you've only dreamed of. I'll show you the sweet oblivion that comes with total submission."

Vanessa's fingertips brushed against Mel's panties. Heat rippled through her.

"And in exchange? You'll be mine, body and mind." Vanessa slid her fingers up and down, pushing Mel's panties between her lips.

Mel stifled a gasp. Was Vanessa going to do this here? As Vanessa's fingers stroked faster under the bar, she found that she didn't care.

"That's right. You belong to me now. And I don't like to share. Which means no one but me is allowed to touch you. Not even yourself. The only release that you're going to get is at my hands. Do you understand?"

Mel nodded, fearing that if she opened her mouth, she wouldn't be able to control what came out.

"Good." Vanessa leaned over and kissed Mel, her lips soft and tinged with whiskey. Then she drew her hand back down Mel's leg, sat back in her chair, and picked up her glass.

Mel blinked. She didn't want Vanessa to stop. She was practically throbbing.

"Unfortunately, I have to go. I have a business trip tomorrow and need to prepare." Vanessa drained the last of her drink. "Which means we won't get to see each other for a little while."

It took a moment for Mel to realize that Vanessa had gotten her all worked up and left her hanging on purpose. And now Vanessa was going to disappear on her?

"Don't look so distraught," Vanessa said. "I promise you, when I get back, the fun will really begin."

"When will you get back?" Mel asked.

"Oh, I don't know. I have a lot to do. It could be a few days. A week. Maybe even longer. And don't forget what I said. No one is to touch you." Vanessa shot Mel a stern look. "I'll know if you break my rules. And I don't want to have to punish you."

Punish me? Mel immediately pictured that crimson-handled riding crop in Vanessa's room. She was sure that whatever punishment Vanessa had in mind would be sweet torture. But Mel wasn't going to defy Vanessa. There was an intrinsic part of her being that needed to obey. And Vanessa knew it.

CHAPTER NINE

Mel flopped down onto her bed, unconcerned that she was still wearing her sweaty running gear. Since Vanessa had gone away, she and Mel had been texting nonstop.

Mel pulled out her phone. Sure enough, there was a message from Vanessa.

How was your run? Did you work off all that pent-up frustration?

Yes, Vanessa. Mel let out an exasperated sigh. She had been in a state of fevered arousal all week. Vanessa's constant reminders were not helping. In the past, Mel could go for weeks, even months without masturbating. But somehow, Vanessa forbidding Mel from touching herself made her want to do so even more. And Vanessa kept sending Mel vague but suggestive hints about what she had planned when she came back. It was maddening.

Mel's phone vibrated in her hand.

Good. Now, where were we? How about hair pulling?

That was an easy one. *Yes.*

Okay. Nipple clamps?

Mel paused and thought for a minute, then replied. *Maybe. And I've thought of another limit.*

Yes?

Fisting. Mel finally wrote.

Which kind?

All kinds! Hard limit!

Okay. Fisting is a hard limit. Another message. *How about whips? Floggers? Paddles? Crops?*

Yes, yes, yes. And definitely yes.

So my suspicions were correct.

Mel smiled. So Vanessa knew how much that riding crop had occupied her mind.

Strap-ons? Vanessa didn't bother to add which end of the strap-on she expected Mel to be on.

Yes. But I've never used one before, she admitted. She'd never done any of this before. Kim, her only ex-girlfriend, had been disgusted by the idea of using even the most vanilla of sex toys. Mel had had other casual partners since then, but she'd never felt comfortable enough with them to ask for what she really wanted.

Noted. I have to go prepare for a meeting. But you've earned a reward for your obedience. You'll receive it shortly. V.

What did that mean? Was Vanessa finally back? Mel wanted to ask, but she knew better. The first time she had asked, Vanessa had told her to be patient. The second time, Vanessa had threatened to punish her if she asked again. Mel wasn't sure whether or not she was joking.

Mel put down her phone and walked into the bathroom. She stripped off her clothes and turned on the shower. Cold water only. As she washed the sweat from her skin, she wondered: did Vanessa expect her to crack? Should Mel want to disobey her to see what Vanessa would do? She was torn between her growing need and her strong compulsion to obey Vanessa.

As Mel was drying herself off, there was a knock on the door. Mel's heart leapt. It had to be Vanessa's 'reward.' She wrapped her towel around herself and hurried to the door.

"Hello, Melanie." The well-dressed woman from the other week stood in her doorway.

"Hi." Mel's eyes were drawn to the package in the woman's hand.

"From Ms. Harper." The woman handed her the box.

"Thanks."

Did this woman know what was going on between Mel and Vanessa? Did she know what was in these packages? She constantly maintained a professional demeanor, so it was hard to tell. She and Vanessa had that in common.

The woman nodded and turned to leave.

"Wait," Mel said.

"Yes?"

"Is Vanessa back from her business trip?" Mel didn't even know who this woman was in relation to Vanessa, but there was a chance that she knew.

"Not yet." The woman said, a hint of a smile in her eyes.

"Oh." Mel considered asking if she knew when Vanessa would be back, but thought better of it. "Thanks."

The woman gave Mel a cordial nod and walked off down the hallway.

Mel raced back into her apartment and sat down on her bed, the black box on her lap. She still felt slightly uncomfortable receiving expensive gifts. But if the last gift was any indication, this one would be as much for Vanessa's benefit as Mel's.

Mel untied the ribbon and lifted the lid. The scent of leather rose from the box. She ripped back the tissue paper. Unsurprisingly, the box contained another set of lingerie. But sitting on top of it were two thick leather cuffs. Mel picked them up. They were black with red lining, and each cuff had a metal ring attached to it. They were the perfect size for Mel's wrists.

Mel's phone buzzed. *Did you receive your reward?*

Yes, Mel wrote back. The timing of the text suggested that Vanessa already knew the answer to her question. Had the woman informed Vanessa that she had made the delivery?

Another message came through. *Try them on. The cuffs too.*

Mel had forgotten all about the lingerie. She pulled the matching bra and panties out of the box. They were made of black lace, so delicate that Mel feared that they would tear at the slightest touch. Both the bra and panties had several thin straps attached at various points around the top and sides. Mel removed her towel and put the lingerie on. It wasn't easy with all the straps. She buckled the cuffs around her wrists snugly.

Mel turned to the mirror. She was surprised by what she saw. Her long dark hair, still damp from the shower, was tied up in a messy bun, leaving her shoulders and chest bare. The straps on the bra crisscrossed across the tops of her breasts. The Brazilian panties covered only the tops of her ass cheeks.

Mel liked the way the lingerie looked on her. She liked

the way it made her feel. Sexy. Powerfully so. Would Vanessa find her irresistible in it? There was something exciting about the idea that she could drive Vanessa wild in her own way.

Another text arrived. *Send me a picture.*

Mel smiled. She snapped a photo in the mirror with her phone and sent it to Vanessa. She waited. A minute passed, then two, then five. Her impatience got the best of her. *Did you get it?*

Yes. You look ravishing. I'm going to enjoy making you come apart. V.

Mel sprawled out on her bed. What naughty things did Vanessa have planned for her? If she closed her eyes, she could almost feel Vanessa's fingertips running along her curves. She could almost smell her perfume and taste her soft lips.

No. The last thing Mel needed was another cold shower. She glanced at her phone. Nothing more from Vanessa. Mel wasn't surprised. That "V." at the end of Vanessa's texts always meant one thing: *this conversation is over.*

The message came the following Sunday morning. Mel had slept in after a late-night shift at The Lounge. She rolled over in a daze and picked her phone up from the nightstand.

Tomorrow night. 8 pm. I'll pick you up. Wear my gifts. And only my gifts.

Mel's heart jumped. *Finally!* Her stomach dropped as she read it again. *Only* her gifts? Did Vanessa expect Mel to leave the house in nothing but lingerie? And *that* lingerie? It barely counted as underwear.

Another text followed a minute later.

You may wear a coat. And shoes. But nothing else.

Mel rolled onto her back, a smile on her face. Finally, her torment would end. Vanessa's mind games were far more potent than any whip.

At least, that was what Mel thought.

$\mathcal{M}$el left her apartment at 7:55 p.m. the next day, keenly aware of how naked she was under her long coat. The leather cuffs peeked out from her sleeves. The day had passed with excruciating slowness. She'd barely been able to concentrate in class.

She stepped out onto the sidewalk. A large black Mercedes Benz was parked out in front of her apartment building. Standing next to it was the sharply dressed dark-haired woman who had delivered Vanessa's gifts. So she was Vanessa's driver. Something told Mel that hand-delivering gifts to her boss's lover in a dodgy part of town wasn't part of the job description. Perhaps Vanessa's expectation that everyone cater to her whims went beyond her sex life.

The driver opened the back door.

"Hello, Melanie." Vanessa sat in the back seat, her legs crossed in front of her. She wore a long, dark coat, and black stockings and heels.

"Hi." Mel hopped into the back seat next to her.

"Thank you, Elena," Vanessa said to the driver.

Elena nodded and shut the door. Shortly afterward, the car pulled out and joined the slow stream of traffic. It was a much smoother ride than Vanessa's convertible.

"Where are you taking me?" Mel asked Vanessa.

"I'm going to show you one of the other clubs I own," Vanessa said.

They were going somewhere public? Mel barely had a thread of clothing on her.

Vanessa read her mind. "Don't worry, it's closed. We'll have the place to ourselves."

Mel sat back. Why would Vanessa be taking her to an empty club? She remembered something that Vanessa had said in her room all those nights ago, that not all of her clubs were as 'respectable' as The Lounge. Was Vanessa taking her to one of those?

Mel looked out through the tinted windows, vainly trying to see where they were going. The privacy screen between the front and back seats blocked her view of the windshield. She sat back in defeat.

"So, Melanie," Vanessa said. "Have you been following my rule?"

"Yes, Vanessa." Mel didn't know when she had started to answer to Vanessa like an obedient schoolgirl. But it seemed to please Vanessa.

"Really? You didn't slip up? Not even once?"

"No, Vanessa." Mel couldn't tell whether Vanessa was pleased or disappointed.

"But did you want to?"

"God, yes."

"That must have been agonizing." Vanessa slid a hand underneath Mel's coat and up the inside of her thigh.

The ache deep inside Mel grew. She closed her eyes.

"Did you think about me while I was gone?" Vanessa brushed her fingertips all the way up between Mel's legs. The thin panties were no barrier to Vanessa's probing fingers. "Did you imagine all the things I'm going to do to you?"

"Yes, Vanessa. Every single day."

"It will be worth the wait. I promise."

Mel bit back a moan. She didn't want to test whether the privacy barrier was soundproof. But Vanessa was doing everything she could to derail her efforts.

"Now I know that you're telling the truth about not touching yourself." Vanessa pressed her finger into the wet spot on Mel's panties. "This is far too easy."

Mel whimpered. If Vanessa wanted to, she could make Mel come in seconds.

The car glided to a stop.

"We're here." Vanessa withdrew her hand and sat back.

Mel flattened out her coat and slowed her breaths. She was beginning to realize that Vanessa torturing her like this was not going to be a one-time occurrence. Elena opened Mel's door. Mel thanked her and stepped out onto the sidewalk. At some point during their drive, they had crossed into a nicer part of town. Mel scanned the shop fronts before her. She wasn't sure what she was looking for.

"Here we are," Vanessa said.

Mel followed the path of Vanessa's eyes. Nestled between two boutiques was a small, black door. There was a sign above the door with a name written on it in red cursive script: *Lilith's Den.*

"It's closed on Mondays. But I have a key." Vanessa

pulled a key out of her purse and unlocked the door. They walked inside. "This is it. Lilith's Den."

Mel looked around in awe. The large space looked like any other nightclub, but in addition to the tables and barstools, there were some unconventional furnishings scattered around the room. A seven-foot-tall wooden cross with small metal rings at each of the ends. A bench that resembled a horse with leather cuffs attached to it. A long, wide table with padding on the top and rings all along the sides which Mel assumed were tie points.

"What is this place?" Mel asked.

"It's a place where people can let go of their inhibitions and explore all of their wildest, darkest dreams," Vanessa said.

Mel's eyes widened. "So, it's some kind of sex club?"

"More of a BDSM club." Vanessa strode into the middle of the empty room. "This is why I'm so private. This is a big part of my lifestyle. Well, not so much these days, but at one point it felt like it was my entire world…"

Vanessa looked off into the distance. For a moment, Mel caught a glimpse of what lay behind Vanessa's veil, but then the usual self-possessed expression returned.

"This is my 'secret.' In addition to a few clubs like The Lounge, I own Lilith's, and several similar establishments in other cities. All separate from my investment firm. I'm not ashamed of my interest in BDSM. But there are a lot of intolerant people out there, especially in my line of work. The gossip and rumors are a distraction. And quite frankly, what I do in my leisure time is no one's business but my own." Vanessa smiled. "So, what do you think?"

"It's nice," Mel liked it more than The Lounge, which she had always found a bit too glitzy. "Really nice."

"Lilith's isn't your average BDSM club. Only the best of everything. Lilith's caters to the same sort of clientele as The Lounge. It's no surprise that the rich and powerful like to exercise their power in other ways."

Mel surveyed the room. There was a set of heavy wooden double doors toward the back of the club. "What's behind those doors?"

"That leads to the private rooms upstairs. And that's where we're headed."

Vanessa took off her coat, revealing a black, form-fitting dress that was cut low enough to be tantalizing while still leaving something to the imagination. And Mel's imagination was running wild.

"But before we go up..." Vanessa looked Mel up and down. "I want to see how my gifts look on you."

Mel untied her coat and slid it off her shoulders. Her skin prickled under Vanessa's smoldering gaze. For a moment, Mel thought that Vanessa was going to tear off the little clothing that Mel still had on and take her then and there.

But Vanessa restrained herself. She wasn't going to deviate from her plans. And it was clear that she did have plans. Mel fiddled with the cuffs at her wrists as Vanessa's eyes did one last lap over Mel's body.

"Follow me," Vanessa said.

Mel followed Vanessa toward the double doors. Half-naked in this huge, empty space, Mel couldn't help but feel exposed. Vanessa pushed open the doors. They made their way up the stairs and were greeted with a long corridor with rows of doors on either side.

Vanessa opened a door at random. "Go ahead. Have a look inside."

Mel peered into the room. The entire floor was essentially one giant bed with pillows thrown around haphazardly. It wasn't hard to figure out what that room was for. Mel opened another door. It looked like a normal bedroom, with a king-sized bed in the middle. But one of the side walls was made up entirely of mirrors.

"They're one-way mirrors," Vanessa said. "There's a viewing room next door. Some people like the taboo of being watched. Others like to watch. All parties have to consent, of course."

Mel wandered down the corridor, opening door after door. There were rooms designed to fulfill every fantasy, from the common to the unusual. There was a classroom, a doctor's office, a jail cell. It was like some sort of kinky hotel.

They reached the end of the hall. Mel stopped in front of a door. Unlike the others, it had a nameplate above it. *The Scarlet Room.* Mel reached out and turned the door handle. It was locked.

"I see you've found The Scarlet Room." Vanessa walked up behind her. She had a key with a red tassel hanging from it in her hand. "You'll get to see what's inside in a moment."

Mel was practically bursting out of her skin. She wanted to see what was behind that door. But she wanted Vanessa even more.

"Before we go in. What's your safe word?"

"Velvet," Mel said.

"Good. Remember, using your safe word isn't a sign of weakness. When you need to use it, use it."

"Okay." The seriousness of Vanessa's expression told Mel that this command was more important than any of the others Vanessa had given her.

"One last thing. Do you trust me?"

"Yes."

"The most important part of all of this is trust. You, trusting that I will keep you safe. And me trusting you to communicate honestly about your limits and what you're thinking and feeling. Do you promise to do that for me?"

"Yes, Vanessa."

"Good. Trust me. Listen to everything I say. And know that I'll be right there by your side the entire time."

Mel nodded. Vanessa unlocked the door, and they entered The Scarlet Room.

CHAPTER ELEVEN

"Welcome to The Scarlet Room," Vanessa said.

Mel looked around. The room resembled a Victorian parlor, complete with red vintage wallpaper and ornate furniture, but with the inclusion of a large four-poster bed. What was on the walls told a different story. The shelves, hooks and cabinets, all held a vast array of BDSM equipment.

What interested Mel the most was a rack on the far wall. It was a cornucopia of whips, including a long, thin riding crop. Unlike the others, the crop had a crimson handle. It was the same one that had hung from Vanessa's bed at The Lounge and had haunted Mel since the day she stepped into that room.

"See something you like?" Vanessa asked.

Mel stared at the rack. "Are you going to use one of these on me?"

"Do you want me to?"

Mel nodded, her pulse quickening.

Vanessa sidled up behind her and draped her arms

around Mel's shoulders. "Say it. Tell me exactly what you want me to do to you."

"Please, Vanessa. I want you to use the riding crop on me."

"Okay. But I plan to do far more with you than that." Vanessa walked to the center of the room and beckoned Mel with a finger. "Come here."

Mel followed, hypnotized by Vanessa's voice. Vanessa took Mel's hands and brought her wrists together. Out of nowhere, Vanessa produced a short chain and clipped the cuffs to each other.

"Raise your arms above your head," Vanessa said.

Mel looked up as she lifted her arms. She was right underneath an elaborate iron chandelier. A long piece of rope dangled from the center of it. Sure enough, Vanessa reached up and tied the rope to the chain at Mel's wrists, leaving her strung up with her arms stretched almost to their limits. Her feet were flat on the floor, but every muscle in her body was taut.

Vanessa cupped Mel's face in her hands. "How do you feel?"

"Fine," Mel remembered Vanessa's words about honesty. "A little anxious. But not in a bad way."

Vanessa kissed Mel gently on the lips. "Trust me."

Vanessa disappeared somewhere behind her. Mel heard the rustle of fabric and turned her head. Vanessa had slipped out of her dress, revealing a lacy black bra and matching panties. Her lace-topped thigh-high stockings were held up by a garter belt. Just the sight of her made Mel ache.

"Eyes forward. Unless you want me to blindfold you?"

"No, Vanessa." Mel snapped her head back around. There was a challenge in Vanessa's voice that Mel didn't dare to test.

"Stay perfectly still."

Mel heard the click of Vanessa's heels on the floor behind her. When Vanessa came back into view, she had the riding crop in her hand. But instead of coming back to Mel, Vanessa went to sit on the end of the bed.

She leaned back and crossed her legs, admiring her handiwork. "You look delectable tied up and waiting for me like that."

Mel tested her restraints. They held fast. And the sturdy chandelier didn't move at all.

Vanessa smiled. "You've been waiting for this, haven't you?"

"Yes." Mel could feel the blood rushing through her veins.

"Yes? Just 'yes?'"

"Yes, Vanessa."

"That's better." Finally, Vanessa stood up. She circled around Mel, trailing her fingers across the back of Mel's thighs.

Mel felt like an insect caught in Vanessa's web. Only she wanted to be eaten.

Vanessa tapped the tip of the crop against her palm. "Do you know why so many people find the combination of pain and pleasure so irresistible?"

"No, Vanessa."

"It's because pain is a stimulant. Just like a drug, it puts your nervous system on high alert, and makes your body hypersensitive in the best possible way."

Something smooth brushed against the back of Mel's neck. She froze. Was it the tip of the riding crop? What was her safe word again? Violet? Velvet. Mel was nowhere near the point of using it. But she found it reassuring all the same.

"Relax," Vanessa said softly.

Mel breathed the tension out of her body. Slowly, Vanessa snaked the riding crop across Mel's back, lower and lower, all the way down to where Mel's thighs met. Mel inhaled sharply as heat spread through her body. The mixture of anticipation and arousal was a heady cocktail.

Vanessa pulled the riding crop away. Mel squeezed her eyes shut, listening for what was to come. She felt like she was at the top of a rollercoaster, waiting for the inevitable drop.

But instead of a forceful strike, Mel felt a firm tap on her ass. The impact made her jump up onto her toes. But it didn't hurt. Vanessa continued, tapping out a series of short, sharp swats with the tip of the riding crop that left a pleasant tingling behind. Murmurs fell from Mel's lips. Slowly, Vanessa increased the intensity. Slowly, Mel's cheeks began to burn. But it only added to the heat between her legs.

Vanessa pressed her body up against Mel's and ran her hands over Mel's stinging cheeks. "That feeling? That rush? It's your body reacting to the perceived danger. Every stroke brings you closer and closer to an elevated state of awareness." She leaned in and whispered into Mel's ear. "And tonight, I'm going to take you all the way there."

Mel heard the whoosh of the riding crop through the air, then felt the sting of the whip on her ass cheek. She hissed.

That was more than a firm tap. Mel reflexively tried to bring her hands down to protect herself, but they were bound above her head. Vanessa snapped the crop against Mel's other cheek. Her skin stung. But it wasn't a bad kind of pain. It was the kind caused her nipples to peak and set her body alight.

"Your skin looks so lovely striped in pink." Vanessa trailed the supple tip of the riding crop over Mel's ass. "How are you doing, Melanie?"

"I'm good," Mel said. "I'm better than good."

Vanessa continued, alternating between gentle brushes of the riding crop and short, sharp stings, gently caressing Mel's body in between. When every inch of her cheeks had been marked by the whip, Vanessa moved on to the back of Mel's thighs. More than once, the crop hit dangerously close to her most sensitive parts.

It was all so delicious. The piercing kiss of the crop. The thrill of not knowing when the whip would fall. The adrenaline coursing through her body. The experience threatened to overwhelm her.

"Do you want more?" Vanessa asked.

"Mmmm." Mel's whole body was alive with energy. "Yes, Vanessa."

"Ask nicely."

"Please, Vanessa. Can I have more?"

"Yes, my pet." Vanessa tipped Mel's chin up with her fingers and kissed her softly. "Don't fight it. Embrace it."

Mel did as Vanessa instructed. She closed her eyes and let everything else fade away. And slowly, she slipped into a state of bliss. She lost track of time. She lost track of everything around her. All that Mel was aware of was her own body, and Vanessa's presence, and the pure, concentrated pleasure that Vanessa was giving her.

The whip disappeared and was replaced by the press of Vanessa's hands. They felt cool against her burning skin. "Do you feel that? The pain has heightened your senses." Vanessa slid a hand up underneath Mel's bra and caressed her breasts. "Every nerve in your body is awake. Every sensation is amplified." She pinched Mel's nipple firmly.

The throbbing deep within Mel intensified. Vanessa's hands roamed her body, teasing, brushing, tickling. Vanessa slid the riding crop between Mel's legs and flicked. Mel gasped. It was like a bolt of lightning shooting straight into her core.

"I'm impressed," Vanessa said. "I thought you'd be begging by now."

Mel's only response was a whimper.

"Do you want me to give you your release?" Vanessa grazed Mel's inner thighs with her fingertips.

Mel nodded. Vanessa slipped her fingers into Mel's panties and between her lips, and strummed her swollen nub, eliciting endless moans from deep within Mel's chest. After going for so long without an orgasm, it didn't take long until Mel was close to the edge.

"Go on," Vanessa said. "Come for me."

Mel convulsed against Vanessa's body, her lips a wide O. She collapsed in Vanessa's arms, overcome by the feeling that she had floated out of her body. "Mmmm..."

Somehow, Mel found herself on the bed, her wrists unbound, Vanessa's arm slung across her small frame. Her body still tingled like her nerves were alight.

"Welcome back," Vanessa said.

"That was incredible," Mel murmured. Was this what Vanessa meant when she said she was going to make Mel come apart? Because she had succeeded.

"That, Melanie, was subspace." Vanessa rolled over to face Mel. "It's a natural high, a rush of adrenaline and endorphins triggered by all the sensations that your body was experiencing. At least, that's the physical side. There's far more to subspace than that. Or so I'm told."

Mel knew exactly what Vanessa was talking about. At that moment when the rest of the world had fallen away was like nothing she'd ever experienced. And the connection she'd felt toward Vanessa had been sublime.

"How are you feeling now?" Vanessa asked.

"I'm good. I'm amazing." Mel reached out toward Vanessa. She was craving the other woman's touch.

Vanessa placed her hand on Mel's side. "Here. Lay on your stomach."

Mel rolled over. Vanessa moved in closer, her body pressed against Mel's side, and ran her hand down to Mel's cheeks. They were covered in angry, red welts. Vanessa traced gentle lines over them with her fingertips while planting soft kisses on the back of Mel's shoulder.

Mel purred. She liked that tender, sweet side of Vanessa. She wondered how often Vanessa let anyone see it. She closed her eyes.

This was by far the best part of her night.

Mel and Vanessa sat in silence as Elena drove them back to

Mel's apartment. Slowly, Mel's high started to fade and exhaustion set in.

"Are you all right?" Vanessa asked.

"Yeah. I'm just really tired all of a sudden."

Vanessa examined Mel with a frown. "You're dropping. Come here." Vanessa pulled Mel into her. "I should have warned you about this too. Subspace can be intense. It isn't uncommon to feel a drop after coming down from it. A drop in mood, in energy, in everything. It doesn't always happen. But when it does, it's my responsibility to look after you. If you start to feel your mood turn, you need to tell me immediately, okay?"

Mel nodded. The car pulled to a stop outside Mel's apartment. Vanessa got out of the car and open Mel's door. As Mel stepped out onto the sidewalk, Vanessa leaned over to say something to Elena through the window. Elena nodded and turned off the car.

"Come on. Let's go." Vanessa gestured toward the door to Mel's building.

As soon as they entered her apartment, Mel was seized by a gnawing in her chest. Suddenly, the prospect of being left alone filled her with dread. In minutes she had gone from feeling blissful and content to feeling raw and vulnerable.

Upon seeing Mel's face, Vanessa's expression softened. "It's hitting you right now, isn't it?"

Mel nodded. She felt like her insides were spilling out.

"You're okay." Vanessa gathered Mel in her arms and planted a kiss on the top of her head. "You'll feel better once you're in bed."

Vanessa tugged off Mel's coat. Mel collapsed onto the

bed and curled up in a ball. Was Vanessa going to leave her now? And why did that suddenly bother her so much?

Vanessa sat down on the edge of the bed and started typing into her phone. "I'm sending Elena home."

Mel watched in surprise as Vanessa kicked off her shoes and shimmied out of her dress.

For the second time that night, Vanessa hopped in the bed beside Mel. "You didn't think I was going to leave you like this, did you?"

Mel opened her mouth to reply, but there was a lump in her throat that she couldn't get words past.

"Oh, Melanie. I'm not going anywhere." Vanessa wrapped her arms around Mel's small frame. "All of these feelings? It's just subdrop. Okay?"

Mel nodded.

"Don't just nod. Tell me that you understand."

"Yes, Vanessa. I understand." Still, Mel hated herself for turning into such a miserable, needy mess. "I'm sorry, I just..." She trailed off.

"Don't apologize. You have nothing to be sorry for. It's completely normal to feel like this. You made yourself deeply vulnerable to someone else. And now that it's all over and things are returning to normal, it's not unusual to feel a sense of emptiness." Vanessa kissed Mel gently on the lips. "Don't be so hard on yourself. You don't have to be strong all the time."

"Yes, I do," Mel murmured. "I've always had to be strong. I don't know how not to be."

"It's simple. All you have to do is close your eyes and let me take some of the weight off your shoulders." Vanessa pulled Mel in closer. "In fact, I'm ordering you to do that right now."

Mel was too tired to do anything but obey. She shut her eyes and put her head on Vanessa's chest, losing herself in the other woman's warmth and softness. Her eyelids began to feel heavy. "Thank you for staying with me."

"You don't need to thank me," Vanessa said quietly. "I would do anything to keep you from hurting."

CHAPTER TWELVE

*M*el woke up the next morning wrapped in a cocoon of sheets, the aroma of coffee and cinnamon hanging in the air. Despite her aching muscles, she felt invigorated. She reached her arm out next to her. The other side of the bed was empty. Suppressing her disappointment, Mel rolled over and picked up her phone up from the nightstand. There was a message from Vanessa.

Had to go. Important meeting. Call me as soon as you wake up. V.

There was a second message sent ten minutes later.

Breakfast is on the counter. Eat something.

Mel sat up groggily and looked across the room to the countertop that functioned as her kitchen. There was a large to-go cup of coffee and a paper bag bearing the logo of the bakery down the road. Vanessa brought her breakfast? Mel backtracked. Vanessa had been here, in Mel's dingy little apartment? And she had stayed the night in Mel's bed?

Mel flopped back down onto her stomach. She twisted her head around to inspect her aching cheeks. Faint bruises were starting to form. The events of last night came flooding back. The car ride. Lilith's Den. The Scarlet Room. And then, Vanessa holding Mel on the bed as she broke down in Vanessa's arms.

Where had all those insecure, needy thoughts and feelings come from? Although Vanessa had said it was normal, Mel couldn't help but feel embarrassed by her momentary weakness. She felt fine now. Amazing, even. She would do it again in a heartbeat, subdrop and all.

Mel looked at her phone. Vanessa's text had been sent less than two hours ago. Would her meeting be over by now? Mel didn't want to interrupt anything, but Vanessa had made it very clear that Mel should call her immediately. Her bossiness should have bothered Mel. It definitely would have, coming from anyone else.

Mel sat up and dialed Vanessa's number.

Vanessa picked up the phone within two rings. "Give me a moment."

Mel heard voices in the background, then the sound of a door closing.

"Melanie. How are you feeling?" Vanessa asked.

"Fine. Is your meeting over?"

"No. But it's nothing that can't wait five minutes."

"I'm sorry, I didn't mean to interrupt," Mel said.

"Don't be. I wouldn't have told you to call me if I didn't mean it. Now, how do you feel? Honestly?"

"Fine. Really. Although I am a bit sore."

Vanessa chuckled softly. It was the first time Mel had heard her laugh. "Well, that's to be expected. How's your mood?"

"Good. I feel great, actually."

"No more subdrop? Sometimes it can linger the next day."

"Nope. I'm back to normal."

"I'm glad." She paused. "I didn't want to leave you alone after last night, but I couldn't get out of this meeting."

"It's okay. I'm fine. Really."

"Have you eaten anything?"

"Not yet, I just woke up."

"As soon as you hang up, I want you to have breakfast. And drink plenty of water. Your body needs to replenish itself after last night."

"Okay."

"I'll talk to you soon."

Mel hung up the phone. The warm, affectionate Vanessa of last night was gone. But she wasn't back to being cool and inscrutable. It was something in between. It made Mel wonder—how much of Vanessa's hard, emotionless persona was an act, and how much of it was actually her?

Mel hopped out of bed and examined Vanessa's breakfast offerings. She didn't know why she was trying to figure Vanessa out. Things between them were supposed to be purely physical. But Mel was beginning to realize that what she and Vanessa were doing together required a level of intimacy that she hadn't anticipated. She remembered Vanessa's words about trust. If life had taught Mel anything, it was that the only person she could rely on was herself.

Mel sighed. Things were starting to spin out of control. If she wasn't careful, it would be too easy for her to lose herself in both Vanessa and BDSM. Because for Mel, the two were inextricably intertwined.

The days that followed only left Mel feeling even more conflicted.

"It's been four days, Jess." Mel lay on the lawn with her friend, soaking in the sun between classes. "And nothing!"

"Why don't you just text her yourself?" Jess asked.

"Because it would be weird. She's the one who always contacts me." Mel knew how flimsy an excuse it was.

"So you're supposed to sit around and wait for her to booty call you?" Jess peered at Mel from over her sunglasses. "That's pretty cold."

"It's not like that. She's not like that."

"Then what is it? Are you sure you're not just afraid of putting yourself out there?"

"Well, maybe a little," Mel said. "It's complicated."

"Only because you're making it complicated. Just call her!"

Mel sighed.

"Besides, she could just be busy. Didn't you say she has a demanding job?"

"Yeah. Maybe you're right." In the past, Vanessa had gone for long periods without contacting Mel because of her busy schedule. But after the intimacy of that night at Lilith's, Mel felt like things between them had changed. That they had grown closer. "Honestly? I'm a little worried that I scared her away. Everything seemed fine when I talked to her the next day, but now..." Mel trailed off. It was all too familiar. She'd gotten too close to someone. She'd shown them her vulnerable side. And then they'd discarded her like she was nothing.

Mel banished her thought. Vanessa wasn't Kim. And this was not a relationship.

"Why do you think you scared Vanessa away? Did something happen?" Jess asked.

"It's hard to explain." Mel considered her friend carefully. Jess wasn't shy when it came to her sex life. And Mel trusted her. "There's more to it than what I told you. Promise me you'll keep an open mind?"

"Sure. I'm as open-minded as they come."

Jess listened silently as Mel described the events of that night. When Mel reached the point when she and Vanessa had gone up to Mel's apartment, Jess interrupted her.

"Oh yeah, subdrop." Jess propped herself up on her elbow. "It makes everyone feel needy and depressed. It's totally normal."

Mel gaped at her.

"What, Vanessa didn't explain it to you?"

"She did. I didn't know you were into that kind of thing."

"Don't look so shocked, Mel. Do you think you're the only girl who likes getting tied up and spanked?" Jess grinned. "Anyway, it sounds like Vanessa knows what she's doing. Aftercare, checking up on you in the morning—it's pretty important. So I doubt something as common as subdrop fazed her. You have nothing to worry about."

"You're probably right." Mel turned to her friend. "So you've experienced it before? Subspace? Subdrop?"

"Yeah, a few times. Not for a while though. Unlike you, I don't have some rich Domme lover who owns a BDSM club." Jess sat upright. "Wait. The club Vanessa took you to. Was it Lilith's Den?"

"Yeah. Do you know of it?" Mel asked.

"Of course. Everyone in the BDSM community has heard of it. But it's very exclusive. I've never been inside. Wow. So Vanessa owns Lilith's." Jess looked off into the distance. "I wish I had a girlfriend like her."

"Just don't tell anyone, all right? She is very private about the fact that she owns the place."

"Yeah, no problem."

"And she's not my girlfriend."

"Right. You just have an intense connection with her, you're exclusively seeing each other, and now you're going crazy because she hasn't texted you in a few days."

"It isn't like that," Mel said. Weren't all those things just part of the kinky game that Mel and Vanessa were playing? Mel suddenly remembered something that Vanessa had said as they drifted off to sleep that night. *I would do anything to keep you from hurting.* Had Vanessa really said that, or was it a dream?

"I wish I had someone who I felt as strongly about as you do with Vanessa. I spent most of my weekend dodging Brett's calls."

"What? I thought you two broke up?"

"That was Brendon. I only just started seeing Brett. He's way hotter. Not much upstairs though."

Mel raised an eyebrow.

"What?" Jess shrugged. "He makes up for it in other ways. It's too bad he's as vanilla as they come."

Mel shook her head. Her phone buzzed. A text message. A slow smile spread across her face.

Tomorrow night. My room at The Lounge. After your shift. Another message followed shortly after. *I'm sorry that I've been out of touch.*

"Lemme guess? Vanessa?"

"Yep," Mel said. Vanessa hadn't given an explanation. But she had apologized. And something told Mel that Vanessa didn't apologize very often.

"Told you." Jess lay back down and pushed up her sunglasses. "Nothing to worry about."

CHAPTER THIRTEEN

"*M*mmm..." Mel lay on the king bed in Vanessa's room above The Lounge, her hot, sweaty limbs tangled with Vanessa's. A pair of handcuffs lay discarded on the bed beside them. Mel closed her eyes and let out a long, slow breath.

The last few hours had silenced all of Mel's doubts. She had been right that the night at Lilith's Den had changed everything between her and Vanessa. Only it was for the better. They were more attuned to each other somehow, more connected. It was subtle but unmistakable.

"What are you smiling about?" Vanessa asked.

"I feel like I'm on top of the world right now." Everything in her life was running smoothly. Law school. Work. Even her modest social life. For the first time in as long as she could remember, she was completely stress-free.

Vanessa smiled and got up from the bed. "Drink?"

"Sure." Mel watched Vanessa walk over to the counter. She still found the sight of Vanessa's soft, white curves mesmerizing. Vanessa poured two glasses of whiskey and returned to the bed. Mel loved the taste of whiskey now. The way that every sip flooded her body with a pleasant warmth reminded her of Vanessa.

Vanessa's phone rang. She looked at her cell, then quickly turned it off. She placed it aside and sat back on the bed.

Again? This seemed to happen a lot. When it did, it was like Vanessa's mask would slip. She'd get a phone call. She'd ignore it. And she'd continue as if whatever it was hadn't bothered her. But she always seemed slightly rattled afterward. Mel couldn't help but wonder what could possibly shake someone like Vanessa. Despite their growing closeness, Vanessa was still mostly a mystery to Mel.

Vanessa reached out and swept a lock of Mel's unruly hair out of her face. "It's your birthday in a few days."

A knot formed in Mel's stomach. "How did you find out?"

"It's in your employee records," Vanessa said. "I couldn't help but take a look. Do you have anything planned?"

"Not really..." Like every other year, Mel had been planning to let the day pass without telling anyone.

"That means I get you all to myself," Vanessa said.

Mel stared down into her lap.

"What's the matter?"

Mel shrugged. "I don't really like birthdays."

"And why not?"

Mel gathered up the satin sheets around her and pulled them into her lap. "They've always been... disappointing for me. It was just me and Mom growing up, and she wasn't very good at that sort of thing. If she remembered at all."

"I'm sorry. That must have been hard," Vanessa said.

"It's no big deal."

"So your birthdays were disappointing in the past. They don't have to be in the future." Vanessa placed her glass down on the nightstand. "Let me give you the birthday you deserve. Let me spoil you."

Mel hesitated. "I don't know…"

"Please?" Vanessa gave Mel a pleading look. Coming from Vanessa, it looked ridiculous.

A smile broke out on Mel's face. "Okay. But nothing over the top."

"Then I'll cancel the helicopter ride."

"Very funny." Mel smoothed out the sheets in her lap. "That was a joke, right?"

Vanessa shrugged. "Maybe." She placed her hand on Mel's. "I promise you. I'm going to make your birthday unforgettable. You'll love it."

Mel sighed. Vanessa had even more of a disarming effect on her than before. But it seemed to Mel that Vanessa was letting her guard down a little too.

Vanessa took Mel's glass and placed it on the nightstand next to her own. "You're the only person I've ever had to beg to let me spoil them." She pushed Mel down by the shoulders, straddled her body and pinned her wrists above her head. "I think you need a reminder of who you belong to."

"Happy birthday, Mel!" James said.

Mel looked at her watch. She hadn't even noticed that it was past midnight. "Thanks," she said quietly. Like

Vanessa, James must have found out from Mel's employee records.

"What are you doing to celebrate?"

"Just spending time with... a friend."

"That's all?" James shook his head. "Why don't you come out for drinks with everyone after we close? Consider it an impromptu birthday party."

"I don't think so. I'm not big on birthdays," Mel said.

"Okay, how about this, I won't even tell anyone it's your birthday. As far as the others will know, it'll just be the usual after-work drinks."

Mel hesitated. She had been working hard lately. And she didn't have class until the afternoon. It couldn't hurt to have a little fun.

"Come on, Mel!" James said. "Just this once. Live a little."

Mel held up her hands in defeat. "Sure. Why not?"

"Great." James leaned down against the bar. "So, how do you feel about dancing?"

"Don't push your luck." Mel grabbed her tray and walked off, knowing she was going to regret her decision in the morning.

A few hours later, they had closed up shop, and James, Mel and a handful of her coworkers were hanging out in a seedy bar a few blocks away from The Lounge. It was one of the few places that was still open.

"Mel!" James yelled. "Dance with me. It'll be *fun*."

"How many drinks have you had, James?" Mel asked.

"Not nearly enough." He stood up. "So, are you coming?" He cocked his head toward the 'dance floor' that the group had made by pushing some tables to the side.

"No thanks," Mel said for the tenth time since they'd arrived. "But you should go ahead and join the others."

"Come on, show me your moves, Mel."

Why did James want her to dance with him so much? Mel let out a heavy sigh. "Look, James. You're a great guy, but I'm not interested in whatever it is that you want…"

James looked at Mel blankly. Then he burst out laughing. "Did you think I was hitting on you?"

Mel's face flushed. "Well, you're always so persistent…" Mel frowned. James was laughing a little too hard.

"Oh, man." His chuckles died off. James sat back down. "Sorry. Believe me, I'm not into you that way. I've just been trying to get you to come out of your shell a bit. You don't talk to anyone at work, so I figured you could use a friend. That's it."

He did have a point. Mel wasn't very sociable when it came to her job.

"Besides, I'm gay." James settled back in his chair. "You of all people should have a much better gaydar."

"What? How do you know that I'm gay?" Mel asked.

"I know about you and Vanessa, Mel."

"How? Did she tell you about us?"

"Nope." James grinned. "But you just did."

Mel cursed under her breath.

"I had my suspicions. Vanessa and I have known each other since she opened The Lounge. She hired me herself. After working with her for so long, we've gotten to know each other pretty well. I figured that there was something going on between you two, but she didn't seem inclined to share, so I didn't press her. You know how private she is."

James and Vanessa were friends? Vanessa never talked

about her friends, but Mel had assumed that they were more like the kind of people who went to The Lounge, not the kind that worked there.

"But it's pretty obvious." James scratched his chin. "After that incident with that asshole customer, Vanessa became very interested in you. She kept asking me questions about you, and would conveniently only come in on nights when you were working. And then she started sneaking you up to her room above The Lounge late at night."

Mel flushed. She thought they were being discreet.

James smiled. "I think you're good for her. She seems happy. She hasn't been in a relationship since Rose."

"Hold up. We are not in a relationship."

He raised an eyebrow. "If you say so."

"I'm serious! We're just having some fun, that's all."

"Okay, okay. You can call it whatever you want."

Mel scowled at him.

James took a gulp of his beer. "So, is she as bossy in bed as she is at work?"

"I am *not* discussing that with you," Mel said. She was saved from further questioning by the return of two of her coworkers, Ella and Christine. She didn't know them very well, but they seemed close to James.

"So, how are things going with Ben?" Ella asked James.

"Ben?" Mel said. "You mean that Ben?" She gestured toward the other end of the bar where Ben was standing.

"Yep," Christine said. "They've been flirting for months. We all saw it coming a mile away."

How had Mel never noticed that there was anything going on between them? As the conversation continued around her, the handful of drinks she'd drank began to kick

BEING HERS

in. And Mel realized that she had been walking around with her head down for a long time now. She looked around. What else had she missed? She barely knew her coworkers. Or had any real friends other than Jess. Was Jess right about Mel shutting everyone out?

"So are you and Ben a couple now?" Mel asked.

"Yes. No." James rubbed his beard. "We haven't talked about it yet."

"James? Are you blushing?" Mel asked.

"No." He crossed his arms.

"See, it's not so fun when you're the one getting interrogated, is it?" Mel said under her breath. Apparently, not quietly enough, because the next thing Mel knew, all the attention was on her.

"What does that mean?" Christine looked at Mel. "Do you have a juicy secret to share, Mel?"

"She sure does." James got up. "Why don't you tell them about it while I go find Ben?" He shot Mel a mischievous look and headed to the bar.

Half an hour and several drinks later, James returned. Ella and Christine had finally left Mel alone after she had given them just enough information about her 'mysterious lover' to sate their curiosity.

"I'm going to kill you, James," Mel said.

"Sorry, Mel." He didn't look the slightest bit apologetic. "Those two are relentless when it comes to gossip. I had to get them off my back."

"You owe me big time."

"That's fair." James sat down across from her.

Mel leaned forward. "You can make it up to me by telling me all about Rose."

"Rose? Did I mention her?"

"You said she was Vanessa's ex. What happened between them?"

James lowered his voice. "It was a while back. I don't remember how they met, or how things started. All I remember was that they were hopelessly in love. You could tell just by looking at them."

"Vanessa? Really?" Mel couldn't imagine Vanessa being overly affectionate like that, especially in public.

"Yep." James was oblivious to the hint of jealousy in Mel's voice. "Vanessa was a different person back then. And they seemed so happy together. But one day, out of nowhere, something happened between them. And then Vanessa basically disappeared for a few weeks. When she came back, she said that she and Rose were done. And that Rose was on her blacklist, and banned from ever coming to The Lounge, or anywhere near Vanessa."

"Wow. Do you know why they broke up?"

"Nope. She refused to tell anyone what happened. But whatever it was, it changed her. She became a bit more reserved, more serious. And since then, she hasn't let anyone get close to her." He took a swig of his drink. "Except for you."

Mel sat back. The world was starting to spin. She tried to sift through everything James had told her in her head, then gave up. She didn't want to think about any of that right now. Mel just wanted to enjoy herself.

Out of nowhere, Ben appeared at the table.

"Hey, Mel." He held out his hand. "Wanna dance?"

Mel grinned at Ben. "Sure, why not?"

"Whoa, seriously?" James said. "I've been trying to get

you to dance this whole time, and Ben asks you once and you say yes? I'm crushed, Mel."

Ben sighed. "Should we take him with us?"

"Probably. Come on." Mel grabbed James's arm and pulled him onto the dance floor.

CHAPTER FOURTEEN

*M*el picked up a pillow and squashed it over her head. Her ears were ringing, and her limbs felt like lead. She groaned. Why had she agreed to go out last night after work?

The last thing she remembered was dragging James onto the dance floor. Everything after that was a blur. Mel rarely drank enough to actually get drunk. She didn't want to end up like her mother. But she had really let loose last night.

The ringing continued. It wasn't in her head. She rolled over to her nightstand and picked up her phone. "Hello?"

"Happy birthday, Melanie," Vanessa said.

"Thanks, Vanessa."

"Still recovering from last night?" There was a hint of amusement in her voice.

"Ughhh." Mel sprawled out on her bed. "How do you know about that?"

"James. I woke up to a long and interesting voicemail from him. He's quite talkative when drunk."

"I noticed." Everything that James had told her about

111

Vanessa came flooding back. It was all too much to process right now.

"I take it you haven't checked your email today?" Vanessa asked.

"Not yet. I just woke up."

"Well, you might want to take a look. I have to go, but I'll see you in the evening."

Mel stretched out her arms with a smile. She was actually looking forward to celebrating her birthday with Vanessa. Then she remembered. "I'm supposed to work."

"No, you're not. I asked James to write you into the roster for tonight so you'd keep it free. You don't actually have a shift."

"How long have you been planning this?" Mel's work schedule came out a couple of weeks in advance. Vanessa hadn't asked her about her birthday until a few days ago.

"Oh, for quite some time now."

Mel sat up and dragged her hands through her hair. Perhaps Vanessa's comment about canceling the helicopter ride wasn't a joke. And she should have felt uncomfortable about Vanessa manipulating her schedule. But she was becoming used to being subject to Vanessa's whims. And she hated to admit it, but in this case, it was kind of sweet.

"I'll see you this evening," Vanessa said.

"Sure." Mel hung up the phone and checked the time. *Crap.* It was 11:55. Mel had slept through her alarm. She leapt out of bed. Her email would have to wait.

Mel made it to campus with a few minutes to spare. It

wasn't until the end of her last class that she remembered to check her email. As she and Jess walked out of the building, Mel took her phone out of her bag and scrolled through her emails. They were mostly junk. Nothing from Vanessa. But she had an email from the Financial Aid Office that had been sent this morning. Had she missed a student loan payment? As she read on, she stopped in her tracks.

"Mel? Is everything okay?" Jess asked.

"Yeah…"

"What is it?"

"My student loans. Someone paid them off. Completely."

"Wow." Jess gaped at her. "Do you think it was Vanessa?"

Mel nodded. It could only be her.

"That's amazing, Mel! Right?"

Mel nodded again. But familiar feelings were brewing inside of her. This was too much. There was no way she could accept this.

"Is it a birthday present? I'm surprised you told her about your birthday."

"I didn't. She figured it out herself. And she has this big evening all planned out, but she won't tell me anything about it." Now that Mel thought about it, Vanessa didn't even tell her where they would meet.

"Sounds like she likes to keep you on your toes…" Jess trailed off, her eyes staring out into the distance.

Mel followed Jess's gaze across the lawn. Vanessa had come to pick her up again. And this time, she was holding an enormous bouquet of yellow and white daffodils. Mel had made an offhand comment about how much she loved daffodils once before. She never expected that Vanessa would remember it.

Mel turned to Jess.

"No. You're not running off this time," Jess said. "I want to meet her."

Mel groaned. She was not prepared for Vanessa and Jess to meet. But Jess didn't care. With a confidence that rivaled Vanessa's, she made a beeline for the parking lot. Mel only just caught up with her before she got to Vanessa.

"Happy birthday, Melanie." Balancing the bouquet in one hand, Vanessa pulled Mel into a long, deep kiss.

Jess coughed quietly to the side. Mel broke off, suddenly conscious of all the students walking past the parking lot.

Vanessa gave Jess a warm smile. "You must be Jess. Melanie has told me all about you."

"Oh, really? Good things I hope?" Jess said.

"Yes, she said you're going to be a formidable lawyer one day."

Mel watched Jess's face turn pink. Apparently, Mel wasn't the only one who Vanessa's charms worked on.

Vanessa turned to Mel and handed her the flowers. "These are for you."

"Thanks. They're beautiful." Mel held them up to her nose and breathed deeply. They smelled as wonderful as they looked.

"So, what do you have planned for Mel's birthday?" Jess asked Vanessa.

"Quite a bit. I'm going to spoil her more than anyone ever has spoiled her before." Vanessa said.

"Well, try to keep her out of trouble," Jess joked.

"I can't make any promises." Vanessa shot Mel a suggestive glance.

Jess smirked, a knowing look on her face.

"Don't you have a bus to catch, Jess?" Mel said. "You know, at the other side of campus?"

"Okay, I get the hint. Have fun tonight." Jess turned back to Vanessa. "It was lovely to meet you."

"The pleasure is mine," Vanessa replied.

Jess giggled. "Bye, *Melanie*. Don't forget about brunch on Sunday. I want to hear all about your evening."

"Okay, bye, Jess," Mel said through gritted teeth. She watched Jess disappear around the corner.

Vanessa walked around the car and opened the passenger side door. "Your friend seems nice."

Mel grumbled wordlessly and sat down.

Vanessa took the flowers from Mel's hands and placed them in the back seat. "Let's get out of here."

———

"Mmmm," Mel set down her fork and leaned back in her chair. "This is delicious."

"Isn't it divine?" Vanessa said. "This is one of the best restaurants in the city. It's very hard to get a table. Luckily, I know the chef."

"You went through all this trouble for me?"

"All I did was call in a favor. It's nothing, really."

"This is *not* nothing."

The small, intimate restaurant was finer than any that Mel had ever been to. From the shiny silver cutlery to the crisp, white tablecloths, everything in the room was pristine and rich. Their dinner, which they were halfway through, ran several courses. And there were no other diners. They had the whole restaurant to themselves.

"And I seem to remember saying 'nothing over the top,'" Mel said. "Is booking out an entire restaurant your idea of low key?"

"Trust me, this isn't over the top," Vanessa replied. "If I had my way, we'd be on a flight to Paris right now."

"You're not even joking, are you?"

"Maybe. Maybe not." Vanessa poured them both another glass of wine, hand-picked by the restaurant's sommelier. The bottle was almost empty already.

"Thank you," Mel said. "For all of this." Mel appreciated being able to spend some one-on-one time with Vanessa that didn't involve Mel getting tied to something. Not that she minded that part. But it was a welcome change of pace.

Vanessa smiled. "Didn't I tell you that you would love it?"

"Yes. You were right."

"Aren't I always?" Vanessa reached across the table and placed her hand on Mel's arm. "See? Sometimes it's worth giving something new a chance."

"I know. It's just hard, you know? To be open to anything new and different after being disappointed so many times." Mel picked up her fork and prodded at her food. "It's silly of me, I know."

"Why do you do that?" Vanessa asked.

"Do what?"

"Dismiss your feelings. Pretend that they aren't important."

"I'm not…" Mel sighed. "It's a habit, I guess. When I was growing up, having any feelings at all was a weakness I could never afford to indulge in. I always felt like I had to be strong all the time because I had no one else I could rely on."

"Where were your parents in all this?" Vanessa asked.

"My dad left when I was young. And my mom didn't like how much I reminded her of my dad. So she basically left me to fend for myself. And she was an alcoholic, so she wasn't exactly reliable. She always found new ways to let me down. And even when she was actually around, she wasn't really present." Mel blinked. She had never told anyone that much about her parents. Not since Kim. And Kim had only used it against her.

"That's awful. I'm sorry. No child deserves to be treated like that."

Mel shrugged. "Well, at the very least it taught me to be independent. And it made me want to escape my dead-end life and make something of myself. It's probably why I'm such a control freak. I've always tried to create a sense of stability to cope with the uncertainty that was around me as a kid."

Vanessa gave Mel a small smile. "We're all products of our upbringing, aren't we? My parents? They had high expectations of me, to the point where they were over-bearing and controlling." She took a sip of her wine. "My father was a mechanic and my mother was a nurse. They spent their entire lives working themselves into the ground. They wanted me to have a better life than they did, so they put a lot of pressure on me to succeed."

"That sounds hard."

"It was. As their only child, they put all their hopes and dreams on me. They loved me, but their love was conditional on me being perfect in every way. So I ended up internalizing their attitudes. I told myself that I had to excel at everything I did. And I sought to control those around me like my parents did to me. Which I clearly haven't outgrown. We're all hostages of our pasts."

They sat in comfortable silence as they waited for the next course. It arrived with another bottle of wine. By the time they had finished with everything but dessert, they were halfway through the second bottle.

Suddenly, Mel remembered. "Vanessa. You paid off my student loans?"

"Yes. It was nothing, really. To be honest, I wasn't sure if it would make you happy, or mad. I know how independent you are."

"It bothered me a little at first. But then I realized I was being irrational," Mel said. "Either that, or your lavish gifts are softening me up."

"Really? Because I've been holding back." Vanessa said. "Next time I'll have Elena drop off a new car for you. Or keys to a bigger apartment."

"I don't think so," Mel said, trying to look as resolute as possible.

"Suit yourself."

"I'm going to keep working at The Lounge," Mel said. She didn't need to anymore. Without loans to pay off, her scholarships would cover most of her living expenses.

"I expected as much," Vanessa said. "If it were up to me, you wouldn't have to work another day in your life. I'd look after you in every way."

Mel raised an eyebrow. "What, like some sort of sugar baby?"

"You would never allow that, would you? You should know, you're the first woman who hasn't simply let me do whatever the hell I want with you. Outside the bedroom, that is." Vanessa lowered her voice. "You have no idea how infuriating it is. It only makes me want you even more."

Mel suppressed a smile. Knowing that she drove Vanessa crazy in her own way was extremely satisfying.

"I do respect you for it, though. I respect anyone who values independence. Besides, I think your friends would miss you if you quit working at The Lounge. James in particular." Vanessa smiled. "You made quite an impression last night."

"Oh god." Mel buried her face in her hands. "What was on the voicemail James left you?"

"Quite a lot. Including something about you all getting kicked out of the bar. He was quite drunk, it was very hard to understand him."

Mel groaned.

"He also gave me a bit of a lecture about you. He went on and on about how amazing you are and told me never to hurt you. I think he's taken quite the liking to you."

Mel felt warmth rise up her face. She wasn't sure what to make of James' sudden protectiveness.

"I assured him that I would never do anything to hurt you. You know that, right?"

There was a softness in Vanessa's eyes that Mel had never seen before. "I…"

The chef approached the table. He was carrying a small, elaborately decorated chocolate cake with several candles and sparklers sticking out of it. He gave them both a warm smile as he placed it on the center of the table, then disappeared back into the kitchen.

Mel stared at the extravagant creation. "Did you do this, Vanessa?"

"I assure you, that was all Joseph." Vanessa sighed. "He's the chef. I had to tell him it was your birthday for us to get the restaurant for the night, but I made him promise not to make a fuss." She glanced down at the cake. "He's been known to come out singing, so I suppose this is him being discreet."

"It looks delicious," Mel said.

Vanessa pushed the cake toward Mel. "Happy birthday."

Mel blew out the candles and watched the sparklers burn down. "This is definitely the best birthday I've ever had."

"It's not over yet," Vanessa said in a smooth, low voice. "I still have one last present for you."

"Oh?" Mel smiled. "What kind of present?"

"You'll find out soon enough." Vanessa slid her bare foot up Mel's leg under the table. "Now hurry up and eat your dessert."

CHAPTER FIFTEEN

"This view is stunning." Mel turned on the spot in the center of the enormous penthouse suite. The glass walls gave a 360-degree view of the city beneath them. The twinkling city lights looked like a reflection of the night sky above. Mel examined the room. There were bottles of champagne in ice on the dining table. Soft fluffy robes hung from hooks on the wall. The huge bed was on a raised platform and looked soft enough to drown in.

"It's breathtaking, isn't it?" Vanessa asked. "I remember how much you enjoyed watching the sunset on that rooftop, so I thought you might like the view here. I called in another favor to get this room. It was worth it, just to see your smile."

Did Vanessa really rent a penthouse suite because she thought I'd like the view? Mel suddenly found herself overwhelmed.

"What's the matter?" Vanessa sat Mel down on the couch.

All of Mel's emotions poured out at once. "All this. The loans, the dinner, the hotel. It's too much…"

"No, it's not." Vanessa took Mel's hand. "Why is it so hard for you to accept things from others? Or to let them in? Do you think you don't deserve love and happiness?"

"No. I..." Mel trailed off.

"Melanie. Look at me." Vanessa looked deep into Mel's eyes. "You deserve the world. And you don't have to go through life alone."

Mel searched the depths of her heart. Vanessa was right. Sometimes Mel did feel like she didn't deserve to be happy. It was a side effect of a childhood spent alone and unloved. But she knew it was irrational. Maybe just for one night, she could let go of all her doubts and insecurities and enjoy the moment. "You're right. I'm being silly." Mel smiled. "Thank you, Vanessa. This was the perfect night."

Vanessa kissed her. Mel laid her head on Vanessa's shoulder and they sat in silence, sinking into each other.

After a while, Mel peered up at Vanessa from under her eyelashes. "Didn't you say you have one more present for me?"

"Are you sure you're up for it?"

Mel planted a fiery kiss on a very surprised Vanessa. "Yes. Definitely."

"You're insatiable." Vanessa pushed Mel down onto the couch and pressed her lips against Mel's.

A low rumble rose from Mel's chest. Vanessa's lips tasted faintly of wine.

She pulled Mel up off the couch and guided her to an open space in front of a large mirror on the wall. Vanessa grabbed the hem of Mel's blouse and drew it up over her head, then tugged Mel's skirt down to the floor. Vanessa ran her fingers over the cups of Mel's lacy, purple bra. "These were my first gift to you." A light smile crossed Vanessa's lips. "I love seeing you in things that are mine."

That was the reaction Mel had been hoping for when she had chosen to wear that set of lingerie. Vanessa didn't need to tell her what to wear, or what to do anymore. Mel could anticipate Vanessa's every impulse without her speaking a word. But she still delighted in following Vanessa's orders. And she loved the satisfaction that her obedience gave the other woman.

"As lovely as you look in this, it's in my way," Vanessa said. She stripped Mel's bra from her body. "Stay right there."

Mel watched in the mirror as Vanessa strode over to the table and opened up a large leather bag that was sitting on top of it. She pulled out several coils of thick, red rope. All up, it was enough to truss up Mel's body from head to toe several times over.

Vanessa returned to her side. "Close your eyes for me. Keep them shut until I tell you to open them. And put your hands behind your back."

Mel obeyed. Vanessa folded Mel's arms against her back, one forearm on top of the other. She wound the rope around the length of Mel's arms in a series of loops and knots. Mel wriggled her arms. She couldn't move them at all. Mel was no stranger to restraints by now, but this was a far higher level of immobilization. Her pulse quickened.

"Are you all right, my pet?"

"Yes, Vanessa." Mel's nerves were more out of excitement than anxiety.

Vanessa kissed Mel on the back of her shoulder. "This will take a while. Try to relax. You'll enjoy it more if you do."

As Vanessa wound the ropes around Mel's torso, she focused her senses on everything around her. The pressure of the soft rope on her skin, tight, but not constricting. Vanessa's hands and fingers on her chest and back. Everywhere Vanessa touched left a faint tingling behind. It was almost sensual. By the time Vanessa was done, Mel felt light and serene.

"Open your eyes," Vanessa said.

Mel looked at herself in the mirror. The red rope criss-crossed over her chest and shoulders and around her breasts. Underneath her bound arms, her back was a mirror image of her front. A length of rope dangled from the center of her chest.

"It's shibari. Japanese rope bondage. Some consider it an art," Vanessa said. "You make a perfect canvas."

"It's beautiful." Mel turned to each side, admiring the snug rope harness that Vanessa had created.

"It is. And very hard to master. It can be dangerous if you do it wrong. But do it right, and the possibilities are endless." Vanessa picked up the rope attached to Mel's chest and pulled on it gently. As Mel tipped toward her, she planted a long, lingering kiss on Mel's lips. Using the rope like a leash, she led Mel up to the bed. Then she pressed her hand into the center of Mel's chest and pushed her backward onto it.

Mel tumbled down onto the bed. She shifted onto her side, taking the weight off her arms, and watched Vanessa pull off her blouse and shimmy out of her skirt. The sight of Vanessa's body, out of reach of Mel's bound hands, made Mel hunger for her even more.

"Close your eyes," Vanessa said. "And don't move."

Once again, Mel closed her eyes and lay there in silence, tied up and waiting for Vanessa. She could hear Vanessa rifling around in the bag again. There was a soft thud as something fell to the table, followed by some sounds that Mel didn't recognize. Just when the temptation to peek became too much, she heard Vanessa's footsteps on the plush carpet coming toward her. Vanessa climbed onto the bed and straddled Mel's body. She felt something hard and cool against her stomach.

"Open your eyes," Vanessa said.

Mel opened her eyes. Vanessa was kneeling over her, naked, her pale red nipples standing up on her ivory breasts. And extending out from between her legs was a smooth, black strap-on.

Before this moment, Mel had never understood the appeal of strap-ons. But seeing Vanessa kneeling above her, the ebony cock contrasting against Vanessa's milky white skin, made Mel throb between her thighs. Nervous anticipation welled up inside her. Somehow, the incongruity between the phallic strap-on and Vanessa's feminine curves made it even hotter.

"Don't worry. I'm going to take it very, very slow. When I'm through with you, you'll be more than ready for me." Vanessa's words sounded more like a threat than reassurance.

Mel lay helpless underneath Vanessa as she made good

on her promise. She teased Mel with her fingers, her lips, her entire body. She pressed her breasts against Mel's. She wrapped her mouth around Mel's nipples, and sucked, and licked, and bit. She slid off Mel's panties and slipped her fingers down to where Mel's thighs met.

Mel moaned softly. By now, Vanessa could read Mel's body without her saying a word. She knew what drove Mel wild. She knew what pushed Mel toward the edge. And she knew how to get Mel just close enough to make her tremble and cry out, without sending her over it. With Vanessa's fingers and lips on Mel's breasts and her hand between Mel's legs, Mel was quickly reduced to a whimpering, panting mess.

Finally, Vanessa guided the strap-on between Mel's lips and ran the smooth shaft up and down her slit.

Mel pushed herself up toward Vanessa. She couldn't take any more of this. "Please, Vanessa. Please! I need you inside me."

Vanessa stopped. She flipped Mel onto her back and planted three firm spanks on her ass cheeks.

Mel gasped.

"Did I ask you to beg, my pet?" Vanessa brushed her fingertips along Mel's stinging skin.

"No, Vanessa," Mel bit her lip. Like most of Vanessa's 'discipline,' this only turned her on even more.

"For that, I should leave you here on the bed, panting and helpless. Would you like that?" Vanessa's soft, sweet tone was at odds with her words.

"No, Vanessa."

"I didn't think so. Don't forget that you belong to me. I decide when you're ready."

"Yes, Vanessa."

"You're very lucky that it's your birthday." Vanessa grabbed the shaft of the strap-on, and slid the tip down between Mel's cheeks, all the way to her entrance.

Mel's breathing grew heavier and heavier. Slowly, Vanessa pushed herself inside, filling Mel completely. Vanessa grabbed Mel's hip and began to thrust in and out, rocking the whole bed with her movements. Jolts of pleasure shot through Mel's body as Vanessa pushed against that sweet spot inside. Mel rose back to meet Vanessa, every movement making the rope harness pull and roll and dig into Mel's skin. Over the creaking of the bed, she could hear Vanessa's own muted murmurs.

Vanessa withdrew and rolled Mel onto her back. "Look at me," she said.

Mel looked up into Vanessa's dark, piercing eyes. They were filled with need.

"Don't close your eyes," Vanessa whispered. "I want to stare into them and see the moment when you come undone."

Vanessa sank into Mel again, sending a shockwave through Mel's body from her core. She rolled her hips, pushing and grinding in time with Vanessa's thrusts, her arms straining and aching under her weight. Their movements became more and more frantic, more fevered. All the while, Mel resisted the reflex to shut her eyes.

Mel locked her legs around Vanessa's waist. All it took was a few more thrusts, and she lost control. She closed her eyes as the heat in her core flared hot and bright and ripped through her entire body.

They both collapsed on the bed, breathless, sweaty, and satisfied.

———

Hours later, Mel stood by the window, gazing out at the city skyline. Vanessa was in the shower rinsing off the sweat they had worked up. Mel reached out and touched the glass. This wasn't just some wonderful dream. It was real.

She couldn't have asked for a better birthday. Sure, the extravagance of it all had been novel and exciting. But what made Mel happy was the fact that for the entire day, Vanessa had made her feel special. Cherished.

Loved.

Mel closed her eyes. She wasn't a kid anymore. The days of her being tossed aside and forgotten were long in the past. It didn't bother her. But Mel couldn't deny that it had hardened her. That over time, she had put up all these walls to protect herself.

And Vanessa was tearing them all down.

Mel heard Vanessa's footsteps across the floor behind her. She watched Vanessa's reflection get closer and closer.

Vanessa draped her arms around Mel's shoulders and pulled Mel back into her. "What's on your mind?"

"Nothing." Mel reached up and placed her hands on Vanessa's. "I'm just happy."

"I'm glad. Your happiness means a lot to me."

Mel's heart fluttered at Vanessa's words.

"There are still a few minutes left of your birthday. Do you have any requests? Anything that's in my power to do, I'll do it."

Mel turned around and looked into Vanessa's eyes. "I just want to hold you."

A gentle smile spread across Vanessa's face, and she pulled Mel toward the bed.

CHAPTER SIXTEEN

*M*el entered the restaurant. She spotted Jess sitting at a table in the corner and made her way over to her friend. Mel had barely sat down before Jess started asking her questions.

"How was your evening with Vanessa?" Jess asked. "Who, by the way, is incredible."

"It was good." Mel looked down at the menu with a smile. "Really good."

"What's that supposed to mean? Did she take you out? Did you stay in? I want details."

"Okay, but I'm going to need coffee first."

"Sure. It's my treat. Consider it a late birthday present."

A waiter came over and took their orders. Mel declined Jess's offer of a mimosa. She'd done enough drinking on her birthday to last the whole month.

Mel recounted the events of the night to Jess, skipping over the more explicit part of the evening. Their meals arrived just as Mel was finishing up. "And the next morning, we stayed in bed talking and watching the sun come up."

Jess said nothing. She had a strange look on her face.

"What? What is it?"

"Well, that all sounds extremely romantic. Are things still 'just physical' between you two?"

"Yes," Mel said. "We agreed from the start that this wasn't going to be a relationship. Neither of us wants that."

"Are you sure? How do you know that Vanessa doesn't want something more? She really seems to care about you. Hell, even the way she looked at you when she came to pick you up the other day seemed like a lot more than just physical attraction."

"I doubt it. We have become a lot closer, but she's still so guarded all the time. Especially when it comes to anything personal." Mel wrapped her hands around her coffee cup. "Whenever we get together, it's always at Vanessa's room in The Lounge, or somewhere else. I've never been to her place. I don't even know where she lives. And she rarely tells me about anything that's going on in her life." Mel recalled those phone calls that Vanessa frequently received that would leave her unsettled.

"You could always, I don't know, talk to her about this stuff," Jess said.

Mel shrugged. "It's not a big deal. I don't want to make something out of nothing."

"If you say so."

Mel attacked her French toast, ignoring Jess's skeptical looks. She hadn't told Jess what really made her feel like Vanessa was holding her at arm's length. When it came to the two of them, Vanessa refused to show the slightest hint of vulnerability. Given the nature of their relationship, it was expected to some extent. And Mel didn't want that to change. She liked being submissive. She liked giving Vanessa all the power. Mel liked belonging to her.

But she wanted something of Vanessa in exchange. She wanted real intimacy. Sure, Vanessa would lavish Mel with affection after a scene. But Mel wanted to touch Vanessa in the heat of things, to feel Vanessa's body react under her fingertips. Mel wanted to hold Vanessa in the height of her own pleasure, at the moment of her release. And Vanessa's release, if only she would permit it. She hadn't since that night at The Lounge that started all this.

Mel put Vanessa out of her mind. "How are things with Brett?"

"We broke up," Jess replied. "I'm seeing Brendon now. We have a date tonight."

"Brendon? The boring guy? Didn't you two break up?"

"Yeah, but we got back together again. He showed up at my place with roses and I just couldn't..." Jess looked off into the distance, a faraway look in her eyes. "I think I'm in love with him."

"That's great, Jess," Mel said. For once, Jess sounded like she actually meant it.

Jess smiled. "Plus, he's not as boring as I thought he was. Turns out he was hiding his kinky side."

Mel shook her head. "I'm glad you've found someone."

"Thanks." She was grinning from ear to ear.

Halfway through brunch, they were interrupted by the chime of Mel's phone. She glanced down at it on the table next to her. It was a message from Vanessa. Mel had been waiting to hear from her all morning.

"Let me guess." Jess said. "Vanessa?"

"Yeah. I'll look at it later." Mel silenced her phone. She didn't want to be rude.

"I knew it. You always get this goofy smile when she messages or calls you. Which seems to be a lot these days."

"It's only because she's been away on business again."

"Oh, so she's checking up on you?"

"It's not like that," Mel said weakly.

"Uh huh. It would save you a lot of trouble if you would just admit that you have feelings for her."

Was Jess right? These days, whenever Mel found herself thinking about Vanessa, it wasn't all the kinky things they did together that played in her mind. It was the little things. The parts of Vanessa that made her, well, her. The faint curve of her lips when she was content. The way Vanessa would sweep Mel's hair out of her face. The way Mel's name rolled off Vanessa's tongue.

The way that despite Mel's best efforts, Vanessa had broken through all her defenses.

Mel sighed. This wasn't supposed to happen. She didn't want to get that close to anyone. The last person she'd given her heart to had used her, and manipulated her, then had tossed her aside like she was nothing. But Vanessa was different, wasn't she?

"Just look at the damn message, Mel," Jess said. "I don't mind."

"Thanks, Jess." Mel grabbed her phone and read Vanessa's message.

"Is everything okay?"

"Yeah. Vanessa just wants to know if I'm free next week Saturday."

"And?" Jess asked.

"Well, usually she just tells me to meet her somewhere or says she's going to come pick me up. She never actually *asks*. And not this far in advance."

"Do you think it means something?"

"I don't know." Mel sent back a message saying that she was free.

The reply came almost immediately. *Good. I'll have Elena send some things over for the occasion.*

Mel frowned. *What's the occasion?*

You'll find out when the time comes. V.

Mel put down her phone. Vanessa was up to her usual games.

"Wow," Jess said. "You've really got it bad."

———

Mel stood out in front of her apartment building, her hands on her knees, breathing hard. She hadn't been for a run in weeks. Between school, work, and Vanessa, she barely had the time. And she hadn't felt the compulsion to run in a while. As she caught her breath, she noticed a black Mercedes Benz parked out the front of her building.

Mel bounded up to her apartment, ignoring her body's protests. Was Vanessa back from her trip? When she reached the top of the stairs, she saw, not Vanessa, but Elena standing at her door. Her disappointment was replaced by excitement when she saw what was in the woman's arms. Elena held several boxes, shopping bags, and an opaque garment bag.

"Hello, Melanie," Elena said.

"Hi, Elena," Mel said between breaths. "How long have you been standing there?"

"Not long." Elena stepped aside as Mel unlocked her door. "These are for you. From Ms. Harper."

Was that a smile? It was hard to tell with Elena. "Thanks." Mel took the boxes from Elena and placed them on the table inside, then returned for the bags.

"I will be picking you up on Saturday at 8:00 p.m.," Elena said.

"Okay. Thanks." Why didn't Vanessa just tell Mel herself?

Elena lingered at the door. "There's something else. Here." She reached into her pocket and produced a business card. She handed it to Mel. "If you ever find yourself in trouble or in need of anything, give me a call. I will find a way to help you. I'm more than Ms. Harper's driver. I'm also something like her personal assistant. So I'm very resourceful."

Mel stared at the card. It had Elena's name and number on it. "Did Vanessa ask you to give this to me?"

"No. But part of my job includes anticipating Ms. Harper's needs. This is me doing that."

Mel stared at Elena blankly.

"How do I put this? You're important to Vanessa. So if I can help you in any way, she would want me to do so. That's why I'm giving you my number."

"Okay." Mel still wasn't quite sure what was going on.

"Good. We understand each other." Elena gave Mel a courteous nod. "I will see you on Saturday." She walked off down the hall.

Mel rushed back into her apartment and threw the bags

down on the bed. She hung the garment bag on the back of the door and drew the zipper down.

"Wow. *Wow.*" Where the hell was Vanessa taking Mel on Saturday?

CHAPTER SEVENTEEN

"So Vanessa still hasn't told you anything about where she's taking you?" Jess piled Mel's brown curls on the top of her head. How she'd managed to curl Mel's hair was a mystery.

"Nope." Since receiving Vanessa's cryptic message, Mel had tried to get the information out of Vanessa, with no success. Vanessa had sent her 'gift delivery' early in the week, leaving Mel with plenty of time to mull over things. Was this just another of her games?

"Well, it has to be somewhere pretty fancy if it calls for all this." Jess stuck another hairpin in Mel's hair.

Mel winced. "She didn't actually tell me to do my hair and makeup. But based on the outfit she gave me, I definitely need to glam up. Thanks for helping me out, by the way. I'm hopeless with this stuff."

"No problem. You should let me do this more often." Jess had brought her huge collection of makeup and hair products with her to Mel's apartment.

"Don't get your hopes up," Mel said.

Jess placed another pin. "All done."

Mel stood up and went to look in the mirror.

"No! You have to put the dress on first."

"Ok, fine. Can you give me a hand?"

Mel slipped out of her robe. If Jess noticed the modest but sexy lingerie Mel was wearing—bought by Vanessa of course—she said nothing. Mel stepped into the dress.

"I still can't believe she bought you an Elie Saab gown." Jess said.

"Am I supposed to know who that is?"

"God, Mel, you're so clueless. Do you even know how much this all cost?"

"Nope. And I don't want to." Mel had gotten to the point where she no longer thought about how much money Vanessa was spending on her. She wanted to enjoy Vanessa's gifts. And she couldn't when she was thinking about how expensive they were.

Jess tugged the zipper all the way to the top. "There you go."

"Can I look now?"

"Go ahead." Jess had a big grin on her face.

When Mel looked in the mirror, she barely recognized the woman standing in front of her. Her hair was piled up on her head in a neat tangle of curls. Her eyes were dark and smoky, and her lips were a lustrous pinkish red. Her dress was breathtaking. The chiffon gown flowed down her shoulders all the way to the floor. The delicate fabric rippled and fluttered with every movement. It was a deep shade of blue that Mel adored. And it fit her perfectly.

"Wow." Mel twirled around in front of the mirror, something she hadn't done since she was six.

"You look amazing!" Jess said. "Vanessa is going to lose it when she sees you."

Mel smiled. She had to admit, she looked pretty hot.

"What about the jewelry?"

"Oh, yeah, I almost forgot." Mel sifted through the pile of bags and boxes which her outfit had come in. She found the jewelry box. It held a pair of silver sapphire earrings and a matching bracelet. Vanessa herself was always wearing sapphires. Mel put them on.

"Is that it?" Jess picked up the empty jewelry box, frowning. "No necklace? That's weird."

"That's everything." Mel's outfit seemed fine as it was. But Jess was the fashion expert.

There was a knock on the door.

"Elena must be here already."

"Elena?" Jess asked.

"Vanessa's driver." Mel hurriedly put on the pair of strappy heels that Vanessa had sent her.

"Of course she has her own driver. No sports car this time?"

"Nope. Vanessa said she had to go early, so she sent Elena to pick me up. I'm meeting her there. Wherever there is." It was all very mysterious. Mel finally got into her heels. She looked around for her purse.

"Here." Jess handed Mel the clutch. "I'll pack everything up and get out of here. I have so much studying to do." Jess grinned. "I guess we've switched places, huh? I'm glad you're finally letting yourself have a bit of fun these days."

"Thanks, Jess. Wish me luck," Mel said.

"You don't need it." Jess hugged her. "Vanessa is clearly head over heels for you."

Mel looked out the car window. They were almost at the outskirts of the city. She located the button to roll down the privacy screen and pressed it.

Elena glanced back at her in the rear-view mirror. "Yes?"

"Where are you taking me?" Mel asked.

"Sorry, Vanessa told me not to say anything. And I'm sure you know how she is about people following her orders." She winked at Mel in the mirror.

Mel flushed, causing Elena to chuckle. Mel decided to change the subject. "How long have you been Vanessa's driver?"

"Five years or so."

"What's it like? Working for her?"

"I enjoy it. She doesn't work me too hard and pays me very well. In exchange, I'm expected to do things that are well outside of my job description whenever she wants me to. Like picking up her dry cleaning. And tracking down things that she wants. Like I said, I'm basically her assistant. But I don't mind. It keeps things interesting."

"You must know her pretty well by now."

"I do. I knew her before I started working for her. Vanessa and my wife are friends."

They chatted away casually. Elena was a woman of few words, but she asked Mel lots of questions and listened intently to her answers. Eventually, the conversation died down and they drove along in silence.

After a while, Elena looked back at Mel. "You know, Vanessa doesn't usually take anyone to these things."

"What things?" Mel asked. They had been driving for almost an hour now. She was getting restless.

"You're about to find out. Look out your window."

Mel rolled down her window. They were on the grounds of a large modern mansion. The white house overlooked a huge, manicured lawn that was dotted with fountains and gardens. As they approached the house, Mel saw that there were groups of people milling around at the entrance. All wore evening gowns and tuxes.

The car stopped at the front of the house. Elena got out and opened the door for Mel, holding out her hand to help Mel out. Mel was grateful. Her heels and floor-length dress weren't easy to move in.

Mel stepped out onto the path and scanned the crowd. *There.* Vanessa was standing near the mansion's entrance, deep in conversation with a pair of older women. She looked so beautiful. Like Mel, Vanessa wore a floor-length gown, as black as her hair, which shimmered silver in the light. Silver heels and jewelry topped off the look. Her dark eyeshadow brought out the blue in her eyes, and her lips were a rich, deep red. Her loose hair flowed down her shoulders in waves.

"Melanie." Vanessa broke away and strolled over to Mel. She placed her hands on Mel's waist and kissed her lightly on the lips.

"Vanessa. You look beautiful," Mel said.

"And you look exquisite." Vanessa looked Mel up and down, drinking her in.

"It's all thanks to you." Mel smoothed down her dress. "I love this dress. The color is gorgeous."

"I thought you might like it. But I'm not talking about the dress. I'm talking about you."

Mel's face grew hot. She had done all manner of kinky things with Vanessa, yet a simple compliment from her made Mel blush like a schoolgirl. She looked around. "What's all this?"

"It's my annual charity fundraiser. Well, it's my company's fundraiser. The city's rich have deep pockets. This is a way to use it for good for once."

"Why did you bring me here?"

"Because I want you here. By my side."

Mel's heart swelled in her chest.

"Here. I have something for you." Vanessa held out a flat square jewelry box. "Open it."

Mel opened the box gingerly. Inside was a thin silver choker. It had a round ring hanging from the front of it, nestled between two small sapphires. It was subtle enough that it appeared to be nothing more than a fashionable necklace. But Mel knew what it was. A collar.

"Do you like it?" Vanessa asked.

Mel traced her fingertips over the necklace. "Yes. I love it."

"Turn around. I'll put it on for you." Vanessa fastened the choker around Mel's neck, the brush of her fingertips making the hairs stand up on Mel's skin. She spun Mel back around. "A perfect fit. It suits you."

Mel reached up to touch the necklace. The ring at the front sat perfectly in the hollow at the base of her neck.

"Let's head inside." Vanessa held out her arm for Mel to hold and they walked toward the building.

They attracted quite a few stares on the way in. To a

crowd filled with wealthy conservatives, two women together was still scandalous enough to turn heads. Vanessa either didn't notice, or didn't care. Mel couldn't stop touching her necklace.

They stepped through the door. The mansion was just as spectacular on the inside. Mel and Vanessa followed the stream of people into a large, packed ballroom. A band played cool jazz from the front of the room. There was a bar to the side, and a silent auction set up in one corner.

Mel didn't get a chance to gawk. As soon as they entered the room, Vanessa was ambushed by guests wanting to talk to her. Vanessa would introduce Mel, then the conversation would move on to business matters. Vanessa occasionally dropped Mel little bits of information, but mercifully didn't expect her to join the conversation. As Vanessa chatted away, Mel simply stood next to Vanessa, luxuriating in it all. The music, the food, the mansion itself. It was magical.

"I hope you didn't find that too boring." Vanessa had fended off the last of the guests. "Politeness requires that I at least make small talk with most of the guests. There are some very important people here tonight."

"I don't mind. I'm happy just being here." *With you,* Mel almost said.

They wandered over to where the silent auction was set up. Mel scanned the prizes. Each was more extravagant than the last. There wasn't a single item going for less than six figures.

Vanessa picked up a brochure for a holiday on a private island in the middle of the Pacific. "How would you like to come on an island getaway, my pet?"

"Seriously?"

"Yes. It's for a good cause after all." Vanessa scribbled an outrageous number on the clipboard. It was by far the highest bid there, and it had to be at least three times what the trip was worth.

Mel's eyes widened. "Vanessa, I couldn't…"

"You can and you will." She put the clipboard back down. "It's already done. We can go during the summer when you're done with your internship."

Mel was both too dumbfounded and excited to reply.

"Come on. Let's go get some air," Vanessa said.

They wandered out through the double doors and into the garden. For what felt like the hundredth time that night, Mel looked around in awe. There were topiaries cut into elaborate shapes and actual marble statues. As they strolled through the garden, they passed an old, worn mirror hanging from a trellis. Catching a glance of her reflection, Mel stopped to admire her necklace.

Vanessa sidled up behind her, her eyes lit with desire. She wrapped her arms around Mel's shoulders, pulling her in close from behind. "You have no idea how long I've wanted to put a collar around your neck." Vanessa's lips brushed Mel's ear as she whispered.

Mel's heart began to race. Vanessa took Mel's chin in her fingers and tilted it to the side. Mel closed her eyes as Vanessa's lips met hers. Vanessa's hot, hungry kisses still made Mel's whole body weak.

"Vanessa? I thought that was you."

Mel opened her eyes. A slender, androgynous looking woman stood next to them. She had delicate, high cheekbones and short blonde hair, and wore a suit that was perfectly tailored to her modest curves. The young woman possessed an air of cool confidence that Mel immediately knew drove every queer woman she came across wild.

"Vicki," Vanessa said flatly. "It's been so long."

"Good to see you too, Vanessa." Vicki raked her eyes down Mel's body and back up again. "Who's your new toy?"

"This is Melanie, my date." Vanessa's jaw was set. "She's not a toy, Vicki."

"Really?" Vicki looked at Vanessa curiously, then turned back to Mel. "Victoria Blake. But you can call me Vicki."

Mel shook Vicki's outstretched hand.

Vicki's eyes fell to the choker around Mel's neck. "That's a very interesting necklace. Did she buy it for you?" Vicki cocked her head toward Vanessa. There was no doubt that Vicki knew exactly what the necklace was.

"Yes, I did," Vanessa said.

"Relax, Vanessa." Vicki flicked a stray strand of hair out of her face. "I'm not going to steal her from you."

"It wouldn't be the first time. Tell me, are you still preying on every new girl who walks into Lilith's?"

"I can't help it. They're just so eager and obedient. It's too easy."

Vanessa shook her head. "You haven't changed one bit, have you, Vic?"

Vicki smiled. "Why would I want to?"

Mel looked from one woman to the other. Were they enjoying this? Mel was beginning to feel very out of the loop. "How do you two know each other?" She asked.

"Your girlfriend here and I are old friends," Vicki said.

Friends? Mel raised an eyebrow.

"We used to walk in a lot of the same circles, so it was

unavoidable, really. Since there are relatively few lesbians on the BDSM scene, our paths crossed quite a bit."

"Our 'paths crossed?' More like we clashed. A lot. Vanessa here was the lesbian scene queen until I came along. She didn't like having a rival."

"This rivalry of ours only existed in your head, Vic."

"You only say that because you lost."

"No, I simply had no desire to participate in your childish games."

As Vanessa and Vicki traded barbs, Mel tried to process everything that the two women were both saying and not saying. Vicki's comments made Mel even more aware of the fact that she knew very little about Vanessa's life outside of their interactions together. She had no idea if Vanessa was still as involved in the BDSM scene as Vicki suggested she once was. She did own Lilith's Den, after all. Mel wondered if she knew Vanessa as well as she thought.

And more confusingly, Vanessa had been unusually possessive of Mel the whole night, even more so just now in front of Vicki. Until now, Vanessa's games of possession and control never went beyond the bedroom. Was this something else entirely? Mel hadn't missed the fact that Vanessa had made no attempt to correct Vicki when she referred to Mel as Vanessa's 'girlfriend.' For a moment, Mel allowed herself to wonder what it would be like to actually be Vanessa's girlfriend.

Vanessa's phone rang. She pulled it out of her purse. "It's the caterers. I have to take this. I'll be back in a moment." Vanessa hesitated. She turned to Vicki, placed a hand firmly on the blonde woman's shoulder, and said something to her too quietly for Mel to hear. Then she walked off into the garden.

As soon as Vanessa was out of earshot, Vicki flashed Mel a charming smile. "So, Vanessa has finally found a pet she wants to keep." She ran her fingers through her short hair. "I can see why."

Mel fidgeted with her necklace. She didn't like the way Vicki was looking at her.

"How did you and Vanessa meet?"

"At The Lounge. I work there."

"Oh? You didn't meet at Lilith's Den?"

"No," Mel said.

"Has she taken you to Lilith's before?" Vicki leaned lazily against the wall.

"We've been there," Mel said, not mentioning that they had gone there when it was closed.

"It's been a long time since I've seen her there. I guess that's because of you."

As quickly as it had come about, the sliver of jealousy that Mel had felt began to fade.

But Vicki didn't stop there. "I wasn't kidding about her being the scene queen. There was a time when Vanessa went to Lilith's every single weekend. I wasn't the only one who trawled Lilith's looking for subs." Vicki brushed some invisible dust off her pristine jacket. "But I've said too much already."

Mel frowned. She knew when she was being baited. "What did Vanessa say to you just now?"

Vicki shrugged. "Just that you were off limits and to behave myself. For some reason, Vanessa seems to think that I can't control myself around pretty little submissive things like you." Vicki gave Mel a penetrating look that rivaled Vanessa's.

Mel crossed her arms and stared back at Vicki, her eyes narrowed.

"Relax. It's clear that you've only got eyes for Vanessa," Vicki said.

Mel looked across the garden to where Vanessa stood. She had hung up her phone and was walking toward them.

"That's my cue to leave." Vicki turned to the mirror on the fence and smoothed down her hair. "There's a girl over there who has been checking me out all night. The man whose arm she was hanging off has finally left her alone. I'm going to go see if she needs rescuing." Vicki turned back to Mel and flashed her a charming smile. "I'll see you around, Melanie."

"Bye."

Vanessa reached Mel as Vicki was leaving. She glared at Vicki's back as she walked away. "That woman…"

"Is everything okay?" Mel asked.

"Yes. It was a small catering mishap. What did Vicki say to you?"

"Nothing much. She just asked how we met and talked a bit about Lilith's."

Wrinkles formed on Vanessa's forehead. Was she worried that Vicki had revealed something about Vanessa that she didn't want Mel to know?

"Vicki said that you stopped going to Lilith's?" Mel wasn't exactly sure what she was asking.

"Yes, I suppose it has been a while. I haven't gone there since I met you. I haven't needed to. Come on. There are some people I'd like you to meet."

Vanessa's affectionate smile made Mel forget all about Vicki's comments. She took Vanessa's arm again. They ate, drank and mingled a little more. Vanessa introduced Mel to more of her friends. Mercifully she seemed on better terms with them than Vicki. Eventually, the winners of the silent auction were announced. Vanessa won the island getaway, which wasn't surprising considering how much she bid on it.

The rest of the night passed by uneventfully. After what seemed like hours, the party began to die down. Vanessa and Mel sat down on the chairs at the edge of the room, watching the hall slowly empty.

"That was quite the night, wasn't it?" Vanessa said.

"Yes, it was wonderful." Mel slumped back in her chair. Her feet ached, and she was ready to fall asleep right there.

"Melanie?"

"Yes?"

Silence. Then, "Come home with me."

"Sure."

"I mean it. Not to my room at The Lounge. Home. To my apartment."

Warmth sprung up in Mel's chest. "Okay."

CHAPTER EIGHTEEN

$\mathcal{M}$el and Vanessa walked through the door of Vanessa's top-floor apartment. Vanessa flicked on the light. Mel barely even glanced at her surroundings. She was far too distracted by the woman standing next to her.

After a moment Mel realized that Vanessa was being unusually quiet. "Are you okay, Vanessa?"

"Yes," Vanessa replied. "It's been a while since I brought anyone back here, that's all."

Since Rose? Mel wondered.

Vanessa turned to Mel. She had a soft smile on her face which seemed to light up her eyes. And for the first time, Mel felt like she could see into their depths. Vanessa drew Mel toward her and kissed her, softly, slowly. It was just like the first time they had kissed, moments before they were swept up in a whirlwind of lust. But this time, there was no urgency. Just a deep longing that only the other could quell.

Their lips and bodies barely parting, they made their way to the bedroom. With a tenderness that Mel had never seen from her, Vanessa slid Mel's dress from her shoulders and let it fall to the floor.

Before Mel could stop herself, her hands were at the straps of Vanessa's dress. "Please?" Her heart thumped hard in her chest. "I want to touch you."

Vanessa touched a finger to Mel's lips and nodded. "Tonight, you don't have to ask."

Mel unzipped Vanessa's dress and slid it from her body. It joined her own on the floor, a heap of black and blue fabric. The rest of their clothing soon joined it.

They tumbled onto the soft bed in a tangle of limbs. Vanessa's scent, rose, and jasmine, and desire, filled Mel's nose. She dissolved into Vanessa's skin, relishing the feel of the other woman's body against her own. Their hands roamed over each other's curves, and their fingers caressed sensitive places.

Vanessa slid her leg between Mel's thighs, and they ground and rocked against each other. Mel's loud gasps were matched by Vanessa's soft ones. It didn't take long for Mel to come apart in Vanessa's arms.

But Mel wanted more. Of Vanessa. Of them. And Mel wanted Vanessa to feel what she felt.

She ran a questing hand down Vanessa's stomach. The way Vanessa's body quivered at her touch was all the encouragement Mel needed. She slid her fingers down to where Vanessa's thighs met, her light strokes eliciting short, sharp sighs from the other woman. The sound was so sweet to Mel's ears. At the same time, Vanessa's own fingers found their way between Mel's legs. It took all of Mel's will to keep her own hand moving.

Mel closed her eyes. It was refreshing to be freed from

their roles, if just for a moment. It wasn't that their roles were an act. They were an innate part of both women's being. But this way, they both got to give and take and everything in between. This way, they both got to let go.

Vanessa began to tremble. Then she arched into Mel, her lips parted in a silent scream. Mel soon followed, descending into an orgasm so heavenly that Mel felt like she left her body.

But they didn't stop. They used every part of themselves to bring each other pleasure. Their mouths, their hands, their skin. Mel lost track of how many times they came. Sometimes separately, sometimes together. The walls between them came tumbling down until Mel didn't know where she ended and where Vanessa began. The entire time, neither of them spoke a single word.

Hours later, Mel and Vanessa lay in bed, wrapped in the soft sheets. The sun was coming up. They hadn't slept all night. They had spent hours making love, which was the only way to describe what they'd done. Then they lay in silence, basking in each other's presence.

Mel brought her hand up to her neck. She was still wearing the necklace Vanessa had given her. A gentle smile spread across her face.

"Melanie? What are you thinking about?" Vanessa asked.

"Just how lucky I am," Mel said.

Vanessa trailed her finger over the curve of Mel's hip. "And here I was thinking the same thing."

Mel couldn't keep her doubt from showing in her eyes.

"You really don't see it, do you?" Vanessa reached out and stroked Mel's hair. "I've been under your spell since that night I took you into my room at The Lounge. When you sat down on my couch, indignant that I'd helped you. I was telling the truth when I said I believed you could have handled it yourself. But I wanted to rescue you. I barely knew you, but I wanted to be the one to save you from hurt."

Mel's heart fluttered.

"All these things I do, all the lengths I go to. It's all to please you." She pushed Mel's hair behind her ear. Her hand lingered on Mel's cheek. "You have far more power over me than you know. I'm yours as much as you are mine."

Mel's breath caught in her chest. Vanessa looked like she wanted to say more.

But the moment passed in silence.

"I'm going to take a bath." Vanessa climbed out from underneath the covers. "Join me?"

"In a minute. I need a glass of water."

"Okay. Help yourself to anything in the kitchen." Vanessa hopped out of the bed and walked off to the bathroom.

Mel lay there for a moment, face down on the bed. Unlike Vanessa's bed above The Lounge, this one was soft and inviting. And the sheets, and the pillows—they all smelled like her. Mel pulled the covers in closer to her. It was just like being in Vanessa's arms.

Mel sighed. Vanessa was waiting for her. She got up out of bed and walked out into the open living area.

Once again, Mel was in awe. It had been dark when she'd arrived last night, and she had been preoccupied. Now, she saw that the enormous apartment was even more impressive in the daylight. It was decorated similarly to Vanessa's room above The Lounge. Here, however, there were touches of warmth. The floorboards were covered in soft rugs. A recliner sat in the corner, a blanket thrown over one of its arms. A well-read paperback sat on the table next to it.

Mel headed to the kitchen and grabbed a glass of water. She decided to take a look around as she drank. She couldn't help herself. This was Vanessa's sanctuary. Mel wanted to find out what it revealed about the woman who for so long had been a mystery to her.

Mel wandered through the apartment, peeking through doorways and marveling at the rooms. An office with floor-to-ceiling shelves filled with books. Another bathroom that was even bigger than the master bath. Several more bedrooms. Most of the doors were thrown open, inviting Mel in to discover their secrets. Mel learned that Vanessa enjoyed classic literature and that she had a large collection of abstract art.

Finally, Mel came to one last door. Unlike the others, it was closed. It had a heavy deadbolt above the door handle. Mel stared at it. What could be in that room that Vanessa wanted to keep hidden away? She reached out to test the doorknob.

No. Mel pulled her hand back. She shouldn't have been snooping in the first place. She wasn't about to try to get into a room that practically screamed 'keep out.' Especially considering that Vanessa was apprehensive about bringing anyone back to her home. Some doors were better left unopened.

Mel made her way to the bathroom. Vanessa was waiting

for her in a tub full of fragrant, foamy water. Her damp hair clung to her head, and her skin was glistening wet.

Vanessa beckoned Mel in with a finger. She slipped into the bath in front of Vanessa and leaned back against her. Mel closed her eyes as Vanessa's arms enveloped her.

CHAPTER NINETEEN

"Hey, Mel. Coming to drinks tonight?" James asked as he passed her.

"Sure." Mel had earned a night off. And it would be her last chance with final exams on the way. Then she'd have to really buckle down.

"Great. By the way, has Ben come in yet?"

"Yep, he's out back."

"Thanks. Do you mind watching the bar for a couple of minutes?"

Mel smiled. "No problem."

James and Ben were now officially a couple, and it was clear from watching them that they were madly in love. They tried their hardest to act professionally at work. But they couldn't help but show their affection for each other. Stolen glances, gentle touches, whispered words. And they lit up in each other's presence.

Did Mel want something like that with Vanessa? The night of the fundraiser had been so perfect. During the week that followed, they'd spent every other night together.

What had happened that first night at Vanessa's apartment never happened again. They had gone back to their regular dynamic. But now, everything seemed so much more intimate. So much sweeter.

Mel fingered the choker around her neck. Vanessa was away for business. And Mel was surprised by how much she missed her. They talked almost every day. And at the end of every phone call, there was a silence filled with words unspoken.

Mel sighed. She hadn't intended for this to happen. And she still wasn't ready to admit what 'this' was. Her old doubts still played in her mind.

"Hi there." A short, curvy brunette leaned down over the bar, her crossed arms framing her generous chest. "I'll have a margarita."

"Coming right up." Mel set about making the drink.

"So." The woman twirled a lock of her hair around her finger. "Does your Master ever let you come out and play?"

Heat rose up Mel's face. This wasn't the first time someone had recognized her necklace for what it was. It didn't surprise her, considering what Vanessa had said about the clientele at The Lounge and Lilith's overlapping. The sly smiles, and subtle nods. They weren't suggestive in any way. They were more a respectful acknowledgment that they both belonged to the same secret club.

But this woman clearly had other motives.

"I don't 'play' with anyone." Mel handed the woman her drink. "And I don't have a Master."

"A Mistress then?" The woman asked.

Mel wiped down the bar in front of her, ignoring her question.

"Wait. Don't tell me. You're one of Vanessa's?"

Mel froze. "Uh, yeah." How did she know? And what did she mean by 'one of?'

"Typical. She always liked recruiting subs at the places she owns."

Mel blinked, then continued wiping down the bar in front of her. She didn't know who this woman was, and she didn't care.

"What, did you think you were special? You're just the latest on a long list of names. I bet Vanessa doesn't even remember half of them. She just uses girls like you until she gets bored and moves on to the next one."

Mel stopped. "What are you talking about? Who are you?"

"I'm Rose. Vanessa and I? We have a long history."

This was Rose? She wasn't what Mel expected. She was older than Vanessa. And Mel couldn't imagine her as a submissive. Everything about her seemed predatory.

But none of that mattered. She was banned from the club.

"You shouldn't be here," Mel said.

"Oh? So you have heard of me? Did Vanessa tell you what happened between us?"

Mel didn't respond. But she didn't call security either.

"She hasn't told you? I'm not surprised, considering what she did to me." The woman took a sip of her drink, never taking her eyes off Mel. "I was just one of her submissives at first. It was nothing serious. But then Vanessa decided that she wanted me all to herself permanently. She even gave me a pretty collar, just like yours. We were together for two years. We were happy. We were in love. At least I thought we were."

Mel waited for Rose to continue. She seemed to have a flair for the dramatic. Which made Mel wonder if she should believe a word that she said.

"But one day, something bad happened to me. Something traumatic. And Vanessa? She couldn't handle it. Or didn't want to." Rose lowered her eyes, her voice cracking. "So she ran. She disappeared. She cut me out of her life like I meant nothing to her."

Mel felt a gnawing in her stomach. Rose's story matched up with what James had told Mel.

"Vanessa abandoned me when I needed her the most. When I was hurting and broken." Rose looked into Mel's eyes. "You know what this kind of relationship does to you. Giving yourself to someone, mind, body, and heart. Trusting them with your entire being. It leaves you fragile and vulnerable. And for Vanessa to take advantage of that, to rip me open and take me apart time and time again, only to leave me to deal with the aftermath all by myself. It was heartless."

Mel spoke up for the first time during Rose's story. "Vanessa would never do that."

"That's what I thought too, until she left me. I don't think she ever loved me, really." Rose's eyes were filled with pain. "She showered me with gifts and said sweet things to me so that I would be her perfect little submissive and satisfy her interminable need for control. She gave me just enough attention so that I felt like she cared about me. But she never really gave me any of herself."

Mel's stomach lurched. Hadn't she had that same thought a million times before?

"She's doing the same to you, isn't she?"

Mel didn't respond.

"Have you ever been to her apartment?"

Mel nodded without thinking.

"That's further than most of the others then. How about her playroom? Has she shown it to you yet?"

Her playroom? Was that what was behind that locked door in her apartment? Mel had been back to Vanessa's apartment a handful of times since the night of the party, and the door had always been shut. Her surprise must have shown on her face.

"Didn't think so. Guess you're not that special to her after all," Rose said.

The sudden edge in Rose's voice shook some sense into Mel. "You need to leave. Now."

"I'll be out of your hair in a second. I just thought that I should warn you." Rose downed the last of her drink. "Vanessa ditched me at the first sign of trouble. And she'll do the same to you."

"Rose?" James's voice rang out from behind Mel. "What the fuck?"

Rose put down her glass, shot Mel a cheeky smile, and disappeared into the crowd.

"Dammit!"

Mel watched James chase after Rose. Was everything that Rose said true? Vanessa never spoke about her exes or her past in general. Was it because she had something to hide?

Was Mel just the latest of Vanessa's disposable subs? She

thought back to her encounter with Vicki at the charity fundraiser. Vanessa had been reluctant to leave Mel alone with Vicki. Was it because she feared Vicki would expose her? Mel remembered Vicki's words.

Vanessa has finally found a pet she wants to keep.

James returned to the bar, his fists clenched at his sides. "I don't know how Rose got past security, but she's gone now. Did she give you any trouble, Mel?"

"No," Mel said. "She just ordered a drink."

"Goddammit. This is the second time that she's gotten in here recently. Vanessa will be pissed."

"Is she really that touchy about Rose?" Mel asked.

"Let me put it this way. Last time Rose got in here, I had to talk Vanessa out of firing the entire security staff. Now I regret not letting her."

Did Vanessa's hostility toward Rose stem from guilt?

"I'm going to have to tell Vanessa about this." James pinched the bridge of his nose. "Look, do you think you could not say anything to Vanessa until I've talked to her? I know you two are close, but I think she should hear it from me since it happened under my watch. I'll call her as soon as she gets back from her business trip."

"Sure." Mel didn't feel good about keeping something from Vanessa. But if Mel told Vanessa that she had met Rose, Vanessa would want to know what Rose had said to her. And Mel wasn't prepared to talk to Vanessa about that. Not until she'd had a chance to process it all.

"Thanks, Mel. I won't mention to Vanessa that Rose spoke to you, I'll leave that to you. I don't want to get in the middle of anything. Just let me talk to her first."

"Okay."

"Thanks, Mel. I'm sorry for putting you in this position." James sighed. "I'm going to go have a chat with security."

Mel watched James disappear into the crowd, a sinking feeling in her stomach. Surely Rose's words were just the angry rantings of a jilted ex?

But Mel couldn't help but think about how everything that Rose said sounded all too familiar.

CHAPTER TWENTY

*I*t had been a month or so into Mel's freshman year. She was at the top of the world. She'd finally left her old life behind. She'd had lots of new experiences. Living in a dorm, going to wild parties, finding friends who she actually fit in with. No one cared that she was gay here. And she wasn't the only one. She'd had her first of many kisses. One of which led to several other firsts, most of them involving the girl in the bed next to her.

Mel turned her head to look at Kim. Her blonde locks were in disarray, and her eyes were closed. She had a satisfied smile on her face. Mel watched Kim's chest rise and fall under the covers.

Kim was Mel's roommate. Over the past few weeks, they had become exceptionally close. And an alcohol-fueled hookup one night had led to them falling into bed with each other over and over again. Mel was infatuated with her.

The problem? Kim was straight as an arrow. At least, that was what Kim said.

Mel sighed. "We can't keep doing this, Kim."

"Why not?" Kim asked, her eyes still closed. "I'm having fun. Aren't you?"

"Well, yeah." The last few weeks had been incredible. But it wasn't because of the sex. It was the little things. The quiet moments that Mel had shared with Kim. Having Netflix marathons in their PJs that lasted until the early hours of the morning. Cuddling in bed and sharing secrets under the covers. Waking up to a gentle kiss from Kim.

"Then what's the problem?" Kim burrowed in close to Mel and pulled the sheet up over them both.

"What is it that we're doing? Do you even like girls?"

Kim shrugged. "I don't know. Does it matter?"

"It does to me," Mel said. "I like you, Kim. A lot."

"Look." Kim looked up at Mel with her big, pale eyes. "I don't know if I like girls, but I do know that I like you. Isn't that what's important?"

"I guess. But is this ever going to go anywhere?"

Kim kissed Mel on the lips. "We don't have to worry about any of that right now. We're young, Mel. This is college. Let's just enjoy ourselves."

Before Mel could respond, Kim pushed her shoulders down onto the bed and straddled her body, leaning down to kiss her again. And within moments, Mel's complaints were forgotten.

Kim woke Mel up with a soft kiss. "Good morning, beautiful."

"Morning," Mel grumbled, still half asleep.

"Aww, did I wake you? Let me make it up to you." Kim

slipped her hand into the bottom of Mel's shirt.

Mel's eyes flew open. "No, Kim. Stop." Mel pushed her away.

"Jeez, what's the matter with you?"

Mel sighed. "I've told you, I don't want to keep doing this."

"That's not what you said last night."

"Last night was a mistake."

Kim pouted at her.

"I'm serious, Kim. I don't want to be your fuck buddy. I want a girlfriend."

"Ugh, that again." Kim rolled her eyes. "Why are you always going on about this, Mel?"

"Because it's important to me."

"But why? What's wrong with the way things are now?"

"Nothing. Nothing has to change, Kim! All I want is for you to acknowledge what this is. Look at us! We're basically a couple already."

Kim didn't deny it. "If you don't want anything to change, then what's the problem?"

Mel wanted to scream. Kim always seemed to miss the point. Or simply refused to see it. "The problem is that I'm falling in love with you, Kim!" There. She said it. "I can't fall in love with someone when they don't even like me enough to want to be my girlfriend! And you can't tell me that you don't have feelings for me too." Mel's confidence was feigned. She wasn't actually sure if Kim shared her feelings. But she hoped that she was right.

"Look, I really like you, Mel. I care about you. And I want to be with you. Isn't that enough? Aren't I enough for you?"

"Kim..."

"If you really cared about me, then something as stupid as a label wouldn't matter."

No. Mel wasn't going to let Kim turn this on her again. Mel steeled herself. "I can't do this anymore, Kim. I'm sorry, but I can't be with you without really *being* with you." Mel got up. "I'll go see the RA tomorrow about moving to a different room."

"Wait, don't leave."

Kim's voice tugged at Mel's heartstrings. She almost lost her resolve. But Mel had caved to her too many times before. She opened the door and left the room.

Mel was sitting in the common room a few hours later when the text came. *Will you be my girlfriend?*

Kim rolled over onto her side and faced the wall. Mel's stomach sank. Kim was in one of those moods again. This seemed to happen more and more these days.

"Is everything okay, Kim?" Mel asked.

"I'm fine." Kim curled up into a ball. "God, why are you always asking me that?"

"Because you don't seem fine. And you're shutting me out again."

"I'm not shutting you out. You're just too suffocating. God, why are you so needy all the time?"

"I'm not-" Mel sighed. "It's just that, you say you love me, but you don't act like it. Sometimes it's like you're only using me for sex. Which doesn't even make sense since the way that you act after we have sex makes me think you hate it. And you hate me." Mel's voice quavered.

"How can you even say that? I'm the only person who has ever stuck by you, who has ever loved you, and this is how you repay me? After everything that I've done for you? I agreed to be your girlfriend just for you, for god's sakes."

"You won't even let me tell anyone that you're my girlfriend. We've been together for six months! And our friends don't even know about us," Mel said.

"We've talked about this. You know how my parents are. If they find out, they'll disown me! Or worse. Is that what you want?"

"No, but-" Mel took a deep breath. "I'm tired of this, Kim. I'm tired of all the fighting. I'm tired of you lashing out at me. I'm tired of all the guilt trips."

"Me? You're the one who's always trying to make me feel guilty. You're the one who's saying that I don't love you. How do you think that makes me feel? I'll never be enough for you, Mel."

"Is it really asking that much to have my girlfriend tell me she loves me once in a while? Or god forbid, show me some affection? I have needs too, you know."

"You want me to tell you that I love you every minute of the day and dote on you all the time? I'm not your mother, Mel. It's not my problem that she never did all those things." Kim scoffed. "And these 'needs' of yours? You mean all that perverted shit you're into? It doesn't take a shrink to figure out why you're so messed up."

Mel winced. This wasn't the first time Kim had used things that Mel told Kim in confidence against her. "That has nothing to do with this!" She threw her arms up in the air. "This is pointless. I'm not putting up with this anymore." Mel turned to leave.

"If you walk out that door, it's over. You'll never be able to find anyone who loves you like I do."

Kim's words hit Mel hard. But she held firm. Mel stormed out the door and slammed it behind her.

She spent the next few days avoiding Kim. Which meant going back to their dorm room as little as possible. When they did run into each other, Kim simply pretended that Mel wasn't there. That was fine with Mel. She wasn't surprised by Kim's behavior. Kim probably thought it was only a matter of time until Mel came crawling back. But as far as Mel was concerned, it was over between them for good.

One night, she came back to her dorm after spending most of the day in the library. She hoped that Kim was asleep since it was so late. But when she opened the door, Kim was sitting on Mel's bed. Her eyes were red and her cheeks were wet with tears.

"I'm sorry Mel," Kim said, her voice cracking. "I didn't mean those things I said."

Mel stood rooted in the doorway. "Kim, I-"

"I need you, Mel!" Kim began to sob. "You're not going to leave me, are you? I can't live without you."

As Mel looked into Kim's pleading eyes, her resolve shattered. "Kim." Mel sat down on the bed next to her girl-friend. "I'll stay. But things have to change. We can't go on like this forever."

"I'll do better, I promise." Kim buried her face in Mel's chest. "I love you, Mel."

"I love you too." Mel hugged her tight.

Mel watched Kim pack the last of her things. Summer was finally here. Everyone was looking forward to it, except for Mel. She was anxious about being away from Kim, especially considering how strained things had been between them for the past few days.

Kim cleared everything from the top of her desk and dumped it into a box with a loud thud.

"Is everything okay, Kim?"

"Yes," she snapped.

They sat in silence as Kim packed the last of her things. Mel had felt like she was walking on eggshells all week. Was Kim upset about going home to her overbearing, conservative family? Or had Mel said or done something to set her off?

"So you're still coming to visit over the summer, right?" Mel asked. Mel wasn't looking forward to going 'home.' Kim's visit was the only thing she had to look forward to.

"Yeah, about that…" Kim sat down on the bed a few feet away from Mel. "I don't think we should do this anymore. We've let things go far enough."

"What? What do you mean?"

"You know, *this*. It was fun while it lasted, but it's run its course."

Mel at Kim blankly.

"Come on, Mel. This was never serious. You had to know that."

Mel's stomach dropped. She knew where Kim was going, but she refused to believe it.

"Of course you didn't." Kim rolled her eyes. "You only

saw what you wanted to see. Think about it."

Was she right? Mel thought about all the times Kim had been hot and cold. How she'd pushed Mel away over and over. How she seemed to only care about sex. Had Mel had ignored all the signs because she was in love with Kim? "No." Mel finally spoke. "No. You told me you loved me a hundred times. You can't tell me that wasn't real."

"I only told you that to get you off my back. Hell, I only agreed to be your girlfriend so you'd stop bothering me about it. It was just so hard to say no to you when you were always so sad and needy all the time. I didn't feel like I had a choice."

"Are you saying you were with me out of pity?"

"Don't look at me like that, Mel. Like I said, it's college. I wanted to experiment. Everyone does this. But I'm not actually into girls. Not that way. You'll probably grow out of it too."

"You're wrong, Kim. This isn't a phase for me. I like girls. I always have. And I love you!"

"Maybe you really do love me. But I never loved you. You knew that. You even said it to me yourself."

No. Could it be true? Had their entire relationship been a lie?

"I'm really sorry, Mel…"

Kim's words all hit Mel at once. She started to cry. Kim was the first girl she'd ever loved. And now, like everyone else in Mel's life, Kim was throwing her away like she meant nothing.

"I gotta go, my ride is leaving soon. I'll see you around, okay?" Kim got up from the bed and left Mel sobbing in their empty dorm room.

$\mathcal{M}$el sat next to Vanessa in the back seat of Vanessa's Mercedes. As soon as she'd returned from her trip, Vanessa had taken Mel to dinner at one of the restaurants she owned. Now, they were on their way to Lilith's Den, for the first time since that night so long ago.

Butterflies filled Mel's stomach. She was excited. But at the same time, she felt a sense of unease. Since Mel's conversation with Rose, the woman's words had played over and over in her head. The time and distance from Vanessa had only made her insecurities fester.

"Are you all right, my pet?" Vanessa asked.

"I'm fine," Mel said. The way Vanessa called her 'my pet' rankled her now.

Vanessa's phone rang. Mel tensed. Was it James calling to tell Vanessa about Rose? Mel had kept her word to him and hadn't said anything about it to Vanessa. Had James called to tell her already? Even if he had, Mel doubted that Vanessa would mention it to her.

Vanessa looked at her phone. She silenced it and shoved it back in her purse. It definitely wasn't James. Vanessa always picked up his calls. It had to be another of those mysterious phone calls that Vanessa always ignored. It was happening a lot lately. And they seemed to get to her even more. At times Mel would find Vanessa gazing off into the distance, her forehead lined with concern. Like right now.

"Is everything okay?" Mel asked.

"Yes." Vanessa snapped out of her trance. "Everything is fine."

"Are you sure? You seem worried."

"Yes. I'm fine." Vanessa's lips were pressed together in a straight line.

Mel wasn't surprised. Vanessa never confided in her in the past. Why would things be any different now?

Vanessa turned to Mel. Her worried expression had been replaced by a hungry look. "I have quite the night planned for us." She slid a hand along Mel's thigh.

Vanessa hadn't told Mel what this elaborate scene she had planned involved. Keeping Mel in the dark was all part of Vanessa's game. And Mel couldn't deny how much the suspense thrilled her.

But Mel couldn't help but notice the timing of Vanessa's shift in mood. Did Vanessa only need Mel to satisfy her need for control? Mel could think of someone else who only needed her for sex. Kim.

Mel pushed the thought out of her mind. Kim had been abusive. Mel knew that now. And Vanessa definitely wasn't. But Vanessa had said from the start that she wasn't looking for a relationship. Neither was Mel at the time. But as they'd gotten closer, Mel had found herself wanting more. And

Mel thought Vanessa did too. What if she was wrong? What if she really was just a toy to Vanessa?

They pulled up out the front of Lilith's. Once they were inside, Vanessa took Mel up to The Scarlet Room. She gave her usual spiel about safe words and trust, and they went inside.

The room looked the same as the last time. But now, there was a high-backed wooden chair in the middle of the room. A small table sat next to it, with a black leather bag on top. Mel recognized the bag. It was the same bag of toys that Vanessa had taken to the hotel room on Mel's birthday.

"Take a seat." Vanessa gestured toward the chair.

Mel sat down. Vanessa pulled a long piece of black cloth out of the bag. Within seconds, it was around Mel's eyes. Vanessa drew the back of her fingers down Mel's cheek. Mel could feel Vanessa's breath and the heat of Vanessa's face, just inches from her own. Her lips parted. Vanessa brushed them with her fingertips, then pulled away.

So it was to be a night of mind games designed to drive Mel into a state of frustration. It was working—but not the way Vanessa intended.

Vanessa traced a finger down to the collar around Mel's neck. "You're all mine tonight. What should I do with you?" Vanessa rifled around in the bag, then dropped something onto the table with a metallic clink. "First, I'm going to make sure you can't escape from that chair. But what then?" Vanessa reached into the bag again.

A buzzing filled the air. A vibrator? Vanessa drew it down Mel's thigh, sending vibrations through her. Mel's hairs stood up on her skin.

"I could torture you with pleasure until you begged for

mercy. Or—" Vanessa brushed something along Mel's arm "—I could punish you with this."

Was it a flogger? Mel liked the sound of that. She wanted something physical. Something visceral. Something to drown out everything else she was feeling. She knew it was wrong. But she didn't stop Vanessa. She wanted to feel the rush to take her mind off everything.

"Is that what you want?" Vanessa trailed the flogger along her thigh.

"Yes," Mel replied.

"'Yes?' Yes, who?"

"Yes, Vanessa."

Silence filled the room. Neither of them moved.

"No." Vanessa pulled the blindfold from Mel's eyes.

Mel squinted in the light. "I didn't say to stop."

"I don't care."

Mel let out a frustrated groan.

"Velvet," Vanessa said.

Mel froze. She had never once used her safe word. But it had been drummed into her head that it meant that everything stopped. She sighed. She knew that Vanessa had been right to end things. This all felt so wrong.

Vanessa went over to the bed and sat down. "Come. Sit."

Mel obeyed. Tension hung in the air. And now, it wasn't just coming from Mel.

"Melanie." Vanessa's voice shook. "What the hell is going on?"

"Nothing." Vanessa wasn't the only one who got to refuse to share her feelings.

"Fine. If you don't want to talk, then you're going to

listen. Because this? Whatever it was that you just pulled? It's unacceptable."

"Unacceptable? I'm not a child, Vanessa," Mel snapped. "Don't speak to me like one."

"Are you sure? Because you're behaving like a child right now."

Mel knew Vanessa was right. But she remained silent.

"Christ, Melanie!" Vanessa got up and started pacing next to the bed. "This isn't a game! You know better than to come in here like this. Angry. Reckless. Do you have any idea how dangerous all of this is? Especially if you're in the wrong state of mind?"

All the feelings that had been festering inside of Mel began to boil over. "You're the one who's always using this as an outlet for dealing with your own goddamn problems, whatever they are. Do you think I haven't noticed that every time you get upset, you assert your dominance over me in order to feel better?"

Vanessa's face turned red. "That's different, Melanie, and you know it. I'm in control of myself at all times. Right now? You're clearly not. And that makes people do stupid things. Like push themselves harder than they should. Like ignore their limits. That's how accidents happen, Melanie. That's how people get hurt."

Mel felt a pang of guilt.

"And you do not pull this shit on me. Do you have any idea the position you're putting me in? I was about to cuff you to a chair for god's sake. I had a whip in my hands, Melanie. Do you have any idea how easy it is for me to hurt you if we're not careful?" Vanessa's voice shook. "Do you have any idea what it's like to live with that sort of guilt?"

"I just-"

"Just what, Melanie? What could possibly make you behave this way?" Vanessa crossed her arms. "Well? Tell me."

"Is that an order, or do I have a choice?"

Vanessa's eyes filled with hurt. "When have I ever made you feel like you don't have a choice?" Vanessa sat down. "Melanie. Talk to me. What's the matter?"

Mel spat out the first thing that came into her head. "Those phone calls you keep getting. Why won't you tell me what they're about? Why are you so touchy about them?"

"What? That has nothing to do with you." She looked at Mel with narrowed eyes. "What's this really about?"

"You're always keeping me at arm's length. You never let me in. And you expect me to become vulnerable to you time and time again, but you never give me any of yourself." Mel couldn't stop her thoughts from spilling out. "You're always going on and on about trust. Do you even trust me?"

"Melanie-"

"Or is this all just a game? Do I mean nothing to you?"

"What makes you think that? Where is this coming from?"

"Do you care about me at all? Or am I just some toy, like Vicki said? Something for you to use up and throw away? Just like all the others?"

The color drained from Vanessa's face.

"Just like Rose?"

Vanessa recoiled.

And Mel knew that she had gone too far.

"Get out," Vanessa said coldly. "Now."

Mel ran out of the room, slamming the door shut behind her. Somehow, she found herself out on the street. Elena was waiting outside for both of them. Mel streaked past her, her eyes full of tears, ignoring Elena's yells.

When Mel got home, she took off the necklace that Vanessa gave her and tossed it deep into the bottom drawer of her dresser.

CHAPTER TWENTY-TWO

*M*el stood by the bar at The Lounge. It had been two weeks since that fight with Vanessa. Two weeks, and Mel hadn't heard a thing from her. That was long enough for Mel to know that things between the two of them were damaged beyond repair.

Mel didn't even want to repair them. Not after the way Vanessa had treated her. Mel knew she wasn't innocent in all of this. But Vanessa? She had kicked Mel to the curb, then had disappeared. After three days, Mel's regret overwhelmed her. She'd pushed her pride aside and called Vanessa, fully prepared to apologize and talk things out. But it rang and rang until it went to voicemail. Mel didn't try to contact her again. If Vanessa wanted to talk to her, she would. But she didn't even try.

Mel should have known that it was all too good to be true. She was done. She'd gotten this far in life on her own. She didn't need anyone else.

"That's it," James said. "I can't stay out of this any longer."

Mel crossed her arms. "Do you really have to do this,

James?" Mel knew that James didn't deserve her ire. But she didn't care.

"Yes. We do." He threw his arms up in the air. "What the hell happened between you and Vanessa, Mel? You've been moping around here like a piece of you died. And I haven't seen Vanessa like this since, well, Rose."

So James had seen Vanessa. That meant that Vanessa hadn't completely disappeared. She was just avoiding Mel.

"Look, I know that you two had a fight. But have you even talked about whatever it is that happened?"

Mel shrugged.

"Wait. Don't tell me that Rose caused this. Did something happen the day that she came in?" James took Mel's silence as confirmation. "Look, I still don't know what happened between Rose and Vanessa, but I pieced together enough to know that you can't trust her. Especially when it comes to Vanessa."

"It wasn't Rose." It wasn't only Rose. Vicki had said the same thing. And Vanessa hadn't denied any of it.

James let out a frustrated groan. "Don't you see it, Mel? You're both exactly the same. Too stubborn to say what you're really feeling. Afraid of getting your heart broken. Just talk to her, Mel. I'm sure you can work things out."

"It's over between us, okay, James?" Mel yelled. "I don't want to work things out. I don't want to talk to her. I don't want to see her ever again!"

"Looks like you don't have a choice." He was looking over Mel's shoulder.

Mel turned. Vanessa was walking toward them. Mel sighed.

"Talk to her, Mel. Your shift is almost over, anyway. Go." James walked off into the back.

Vanessa reached the bar. "Hi," Vanessa said. "Can we talk?"

"There's nothing to talk about." Mel turned away and began tidying up behind the bar.

"I need to tell you the truth, Melanie. About everything. About Rose."

Mel hesitated.

"Please, Melanie."

Mel balled her fists. She had never been able to resist Vanessa's pleas. "Fine."

A few minutes later, they were seated at a booth at the quieter end of the club. A generous glass of whiskey sat before each of them. Vanessa had insisted on it. Mel was begrudgingly grateful.

Vanessa took a long drink. She placed her glass down on the table. "I'm so sorry, Melanie. For the way that I treated you that night. For disappearing." She paused. "I'm sorry. I'm...not very good at this. This is hard."

"This is hard? For you?" Mel's voice cracked. "It's been two weeks, Vanessa. Two fucking weeks since you yelled at me and told me to leave. And then nothing!"

"I know. I'm sorry."

"I tried to call you." Hot tears formed in the corners of Mel's eyes.

"I know. I'm so sorry, Melanie. I was in a bad place and..." Vanessa closed her eyes for a moment. "I can explain. Or at least, I can try to."

Mel crossed her arms. Nothing that Vanessa could say would make her change her mind.

"James told me that Rose came in here. He omitted the fact that she'd spoken to you until I pressed him. You never said anything." She looked into Mel's eyes searchingly, but Mel's face was stone. "It was no coincidence that Rose came in here and spoke to you. She must have heard about you after I took you to the fundraiser. People gossip. Word gets around. She probably got jealous and decided to sabotage things. She's like that. And for the past few weeks, she's been... well, she's the reason I've been so distracted lately."

For the first time, Mel noticed that Vanessa looked different. She was wearing jeans. A plain blouse. No makeup. Her hair was pulled back into a messy ponytail instead of loose over her shoulders like usual. It was a far cry from the impeccably put-together woman Mel knew.

"I'll start at the beginning. I'll start with what really happened with Rose. I didn't abandon her, Melanie. I ended things because she was careless about her limits. And it nearly killed her."

Mel watched Vanessa take another drink. She was clearly struggling with this. Mel owed it to Vanessa to hear her out.

"I met Rose years ago at Lilith's Den. We were instantly drawn to each other. We were both deep into the BDSM scene at the time, her even more so than me. She was older and more experienced, which was why I never expected that things could go so wrong..." She trailed off, a distant look in her eyes. "It started as the two of us just having fun together. Then, she became my submissive. And eventually, we fell in love, and she became my girlfriend too. It was the first and last time I had ever mixed love and BDSM."

Mel felt a twinge of jealousy, but pushed it away.

"Rose was a BDSM junkie. She was always chasing that high. She loved bondage more than anything. I learned shibari for her."

Mel thought back to her birthday when Vanessa had bound her up in all those knots. It only aggravated her even more.

Vanessa pressed on. "Over time, the things that she wanted us to do together became more and more extreme. There were many occasions when I refused to do something she wanted because I felt it was too risky. But Rose would keep pushing. Sometimes I held firm, but occasionally I gave in." A wistful look crossed her face. "I've never been good at saying no to the people I love. I just want so much to make them happy."

Vanessa's words from that night after the fundraiser echoed in Mel's mind. *All these things I do, all the lengths I go to. It's all to please you.*

"There were so many red flags. Rose was irresponsible and reckless from the start. She was always pushing limits in every area of her life and our relationship. She didn't take things seriously. Didn't respect my boundaries or her own. But I ignored the signs because I was in love with her."

Mel couldn't help but empathize. She knew what it was like to be blind to someone's faults because of love.

"It's no excuse, of course. Her safety was my responsibility. I should never have done anything I felt uncomfortable with. But one day, I agreed to do a very complex scene with her. Rose wanted to be tied up, gagged, and suspended from the ceiling. Suspension bondage is not for beginners. By then, I was experienced enough that I felt confident doing something like that. But no amount of experience changes the fact that if anything goes wrong, getting out of all those bonds is a long and difficult process. And it requires an incredible amount of trust on both sides. Which, until that point, I thought we had." Vanessa stared down into her glass. "But there was something that Rose had kept from me. And I found out about it in the worst possible way."

Mel watched Vanessa as she gulped down the last of her drink.

"We were at my apartment. In the playroom. I had tied Rose up in a way that immobilized her entire body, and I suspended her from the ceiling, just like she wanted. I was teasing her with a flogger. She had a gag in her mouth which made it difficult for her to communicate. But we had come up with signs for situations like that. Simple signs she could make with her hands, for things like 'I'm okay,' 'stop,' and her safe word. Rose had given me the okay several times. Everything was going well. Suddenly, she started gasping for air. Like she couldn't breathe. And she was shaking, and crying, and..." Vanessa's voice was so quiet that Mel could barely hear her. "I'll never forget the look in her eyes. She thought she was going to die. And maybe she would have if I hadn't acted quickly. I took the gag from her mouth and cut her down. I always kept scissors nearby just in case, but I didn't think I'd ever need them. It took far too long to get her out of all the ropes. Those seconds, they felt like hours. I didn't know what was happening to her. I called 911, frantic. And I held her until the ambulance arrived."

The pain in Vanessa's voice made Mel's heart ache.

"They took her to the hospital. They treated her. She was fine in the end. But I didn't know this at the time because I was detained by the police at the hospital. The scene that the paramedics were faced with when they walked into my apartment must have looked suspicious from the outside. Not to mention all the marks on Rose's body. The police had questions for me. They interrogated me about my relationship with Rose as if they didn't believe that I was her girlfriend of two years. They took the fact that I didn't even know about Rose's condition to mean that our relationship wasn't what I said it was. Because I should have known if I was that close to her. It took several hours and a phone call from my lawyer to clear it all up. And once I was released, Rose told me the truth."

"She'd had asthma her entire life. Serious asthma that had her in and out of the hospital. No one ever thinks of asthma as something that can be life-threatening. But it was for Rose. It almost killed her as a child on a few occasions. It was very traumatic for her. I think those memories are what had her so afraid that day in my playroom when she started to have trouble breathing..." Vanessa gripped her empty glass, her knuckles white. "Rose said that her asthma improved as she got older. She still had to take medication for it daily. And she still occasionally had attacks. But she hid it from everyone, including me. I don't know why. Perhaps she deliberately kept it from me because she knew that I would never do anything extreme with her if I knew. Or perhaps she was just in denial about how serious her condition was.

"But her secrecy made everything so much worse. She had an inhaler in her purse the entire time. It was on the coffee table, just a few feet from the playroom door. But I didn't know it was there. And she was too incoherent to tell me about it. It wasn't just the asthma. All the adrenaline running through her veins seemed to trigger a panic attack, which made everything worse. Not to mention she was already deep in subspace. You know what it's like when you're there. How detached you feel from reality, how hard it is to think, to feel."

Mel knew Vanessa was right about that. It would be terrifying to have something go wrong while in that headspace.

"That incident shook us both to the core. I know in my head that what happened wasn't my fault, but in my heart I can't stop feeling like I failed to protect her." Vanessa's eyes were wet with tears. But she wouldn't let them fall. "Rose wanted to keep going. To continue with our life, our relationship, like nothing had happened. I tried. But I just couldn't do it. Every time I looked at her it was a reminder of how I let love cloud my judgment and nearly killed someone I loved. So I ended things with her.

"She didn't take it well. She'd show up at all the places she knew I'd be and beg me to take her back. But I couldn't let it happen again. So I locked that playroom door forever. And I locked up my heart forever. I banned her from all the places I owned, hoping it would keep her away.

"But it didn't stop her. She kept calling me, begging me to take her back. Eventually, she stopped. I thought that was the end of it. But now and then, for whatever reason, she starts again. The phone calls I keep getting that I never answer? They're not from work. They're from her."

Mel spoke for the first time during Vanessa's long confession. "Why do you put up with it? You could have changed your number, you could have blocked her. You don't even answer her calls." Mel didn't mean to sound like she was blaming Vanessa, although she likely did. She just couldn't understand why someone as strong as Vanessa would allow Rose to hold her hostage all this time.

"Because I know her. I've seen firsthand the lengths she was willing to go to get me back. It bordered on stalking. So when it stopped, and all that was left was her calling me once in a while? I was relieved. I figured that if this was all I had to deal with I could handle it. And I think there was a part of me that saw it as a kind of penance."

Mel's surprise turned into empathy. She knew what it was like to feel the guilt of something that wasn't your fault. Her father leaving. Her mother's resentment toward her. Kim's unpredictable anger. She knew now that none of it was her fault. But it didn't stop her from feeling like it was.

Vanessa picked up her glass to drink and saw that it was empty. She placed it back down and sighed. "It doesn't matter. Rose ended up escalating her behavior again in the end. The night that she came into The Lounge and spoke to you wasn't the first time she'd tried to slip past security recently. That night long ago when I came in to see you and ran off after talking to James? It was because she'd tried to get into the club just hours before. I was far too shaken to talk to you for the rest of the night. I never did apologize to you for that." Vanessa smiled weakly. "It seems silly in comparison now."

Mel didn't know what to say. She had no idea that any of this was going on.

"Everything with Rose? It happened years ago. And it took a long time for me to get over it. Initially, I stayed away from BDSM altogether. But eventually, I found myself back at Lilith's. And since then there have been other women, some of them submissives. And yes, there were a lot of them. I suppose I gained a reputation because of it, which is what Vicki hinted at when she spoke to you. I'm not proud of the way I behaved. But it was all because I didn't want anyone to get too close. I felt that if I developed feelings for them, I couldn't trust myself to be responsible. So I cut them loose before they could get too attached." Vanessa looked up at Mel. "But then I met you."

Mel's heart skipped a beat. The sudden affection in Vanessa's eyes made her resolve waver.

"I never intended to start anything with you. But I couldn't help it. I was drawn to you. That night in the Scarlet Room, the first time I took you to Lilith's Den? That was when I realized I was falling for you. And it terrified me. I considered ending things. But I couldn't stay away."

Mel thought back to when she had been agonizing over whether she had scared Vanessa off. She had been wrong about the reason, but at least now she knew it wasn't all in her imagination.

"And that night two weeks ago at Lilith's when you were angry with me. It reminded me far too much of the way Rose used to push boundaries. And once again, I found myself in a position where someone I cared about was behaving recklessly in a situation where I could potentially hurt them. That's why I reacted the way I did. And when you said Rose's name? I fell apart. I couldn't handle being reminded of how I'd failed to keep her safe."

Mel suddenly remembered something that Vanessa had said the night of their fight at Lilith's. *Do you have any idea what it's like to live with that sort of guilt?* Mel felt sick to her stomach. She hadn't caught it back then, but now it all made sense. And she'd made it so much worse by throwing Rose's name at Vanessa without knowing the gravity it held. The horror of what she'd done and said hit her at once.

"So I pushed you away. I shut the world out. I got lost in my own head. Which is why it took me so long to realize that I'd done the one thing you feared more than anything."

Mel looked down, her vision blurring with tears.

"Oh, Melanie. I'm so sorry. For lashing out at you, for disappearing when I should have been there. I never meant to abandon you. I need you to know that." Vanessa took Mel's hand across the table. "I will never leave you again, Melanie. You mean more to me than you could ever know."

Mel's heart slowed. Vanessa's hand felt heavy in hers. She looked into Vanessa's eyes. "I'm sorry, Vanessa. All those things that I did, all those things that I said to you—I had no idea. I should never have said any of it. I was angry, and careless, and stupid." Mel wanted to say that everything was fine now. That they could just go back to the way things were. But Mel was far too overwhelmed by everything. So she did what she always did. She retreated. "I just… I can't. I'm sorry. I can't do this." Mel pulled her hand away.

"Melanie, wait…"

"Goodbye, Vanessa." Ignoring the pleading look in Vanessa's eyes, Mel stood up and walked away.

CHAPTER TWENTY-THREE

"That's it for the day, everyone," Professor Carr said. "And for the year. Congratulations on making it through your first year of law school." She crossed her arms and leaned back on her desk. "Don't get too excited. Your second year will make this year seem like kindergarten."

The class broke out into chatter. Mel gathered her things and followed Jess to the door absently. Now that school was over for the year, she had nothing to distract her from what was really on her mind.

"Melanie, can I see you for a moment?" Professor Carr waved Mel over to her desk.

"Sure." Mel told Jess she'd catch up with her later.

"Melanie. How would you like to be my intern this summer?" Professor Carr asked.

"What?" A smile broke out on Mel's face. "Seriously?"

"Yep. Your performance in class impressed me. Plus, you aced your final exam. Top of the class by the way. Congratulations."

"Thanks, Professor."

"So is that a yes?"

"Yes," Mel said. "Of course."

Professor Carr smiled. "I'll be in touch over the next few days. Enjoy your free time while you have it because you're going to be working hard all summer."

"Okay. Thanks, Professor."

Jess was waiting for Mel out in the hall. "So? Did you get the internship?"

"Yep," Mel replied.

"That's great, Mel!"

"Yeah. I guess so." Mel gave Jess a weak smile.

"That's more like it! Let's go out to celebrate. Now that school is over, you have no more excuses. And I know you don't have work tonight."

"I don't know," Mel said. "I just want to go home and relax."

"By relax, do you mean 'sulk about Vanessa?'" Jess asked. "When was the last time you left the house for something other than work or school?"

"I went for a run yesterday." Mel had taken it up again in the past few weeks. She needed the distraction.

"Come on, one drink. I'm not letting you sit around and mope any longer."

"Fine." Mel didn't have the energy to argue.

Half an hour later, Mel and Jess were sitting in a bar a few blocks from campus.

"I can't wait to start at the DA's office," Jess said. She too had gotten the internship she wanted. "It'll probably be lots of paperwork and case research, but I hope I get to see some interesting trials..."

Mel stared into her glass as Jess chatted away. Mel had gotten everything she wanted. She'd ended the year with an amazing GPA, and she'd gotten an internship that most law students would kill for under a woman she idolized. A few months ago that would have made her happy. But instead, she felt empty.

"I need to go shopping," Jess finished the last of her cocktail. "My wardrobe is nowhere near professional enough. Wanna come, Mel?"

"Sure," Mel replied.

"I think I'll go for a whole new look. New clothes, a new hairstyle. The works. I've been thinking about trying a shorter style, what do you think? I asked Brendon, and he just said 'whatever makes you happy.' I appreciate the sentiment, but sometimes I wish he had opinions of his own..."

Mel swirled her drink around in her glass. Whiskey. She'd ordered it without thinking. She pushed her drink away with a sigh. It should have been Vanessa she was celebrating with. Vanessa had asked Mel if she could treat her when she got the internship. Mel had agreed to it, with the caveat that it was 'nothing over the top.'

Mel almost laughed now at the idea of giving Vanessa 'permission' to do something. She felt a tinge of sadness when she thought about the fact that she'd never experience Vanessa spoiling her again. And that she'd never get to go on that island getaway with Vanessa. She'd actually been looking forward to it.

"Still thinking about Vanessa, huh?" Jess said.

Mel nodded.

"What really happened between you two? It might help to talk about it."

"It won't." Mel downed the rest of her whiskey. She hadn't told Jess the details of what happened between her and Vanessa. Not because it was hard to talk about. But because Mel was afraid that Jess would confirm what Mel was now starting to feel. That she was an idiot for walking away from Vanessa.

"Okay. I won't push you." Jess got up. "I'm going to the ladies' room. I'll be back in a minute."

As Jess disappeared into the crowd, Mel pulled out her phone to pass the time. She opened up her social media feed and started to browse. Among the notifications was a friend request.

From Kim Roberts.

Mel's stomach dropped. After Kim had broken up with Mel, she had cut off all ties, deleting Mel from everything as if trying to erase their entire relationship. When they had crossed paths at college the following year, Kim had acted like Mel wasn't even there.

So why did she send this friend request? Why now?

Mel's curiosity got the best of her. She tapped 'accept' and scrolled through Kim's profile. It was mostly pictures of her, looking almost the same as in college. Most of them seemed to be with the same woman. As she scrolled down, the woman showed up over and over again. Mel reached a post announcing Kim's engagement. Kim was getting married to someone named Alex. The post was accompanied by a photo of Kim and the woman who kept popping up in all those photos. Alex. Mel's mouth dropped open. Kim was marrying a woman.

Anger prickled inside her. Kim had dumped Mel

claiming she wasn't into girls, and here she was, marrying another woman? *That hypocrite.*

Mel put her phone down and took a breath. It was unfair to be mad at Kim for that. Kim wouldn't be the first person who had struggled with their sexuality. And it made sense. Kim had grown up with a conservative family. And she'd always seemed to feel guilt and shame when it came to sex. Did this mean that Kim had lied all that time ago when she said she wasn't into girls? And if so, was she lying to Mel or to herself?

As Mel mulled over everything in her mind, something else occurred to her. What other lies had Kim told her? *I'm not into girls. This was never serious.*

I never loved you.

Mel had never gotten over the things that Kim had said to her that day. Not to mention how Kim had treated her throughout their entire relationship. Kim's constant emotional manipulation had made Mel second-guess herself even more than she already did when it came to her feelings. Every time she got close to anyone, she would wonder: *do they actually love me? Will they just leave me like everyone else? Is this what I deserve?*

And Mel had let those stupid, baseless insecurities ruin everything with Vanessa.

She sighed. Mel turning her back on Vanessa after she'd poured her heart out was the final nail in the coffin. It was too late to fix things. And clearly, she was too broken to be in a relationship. Vanessa was better off without her.

Jess returned to the table. Mel turned off her phone and stuffed it in her bag.

"Everything okay?" Jess asked?

"Yep." Mel pushed it all out of her mind. "Let's get another drink."

CHAPTER TWENTY-FOUR

*M*el opened her dresser drawers one by one. Nothing. She let out a groan of frustration. She had to have a few pairs of pantyhose lying around. Her internship started tomorrow, and she needed to look professional. She had to make a good first impression. This internship could lead to a job when she graduated in a few years. She was not going to squander the opportunity.

She smiled to herself. Things were starting to look up. Mel had a chance to do some good at The LSP, even if that just meant going on coffee runs for the lawyers who were doing the real work. And working with Professor Carr outside of the classroom would be an invaluable experience. There was a world of possibilities ahead of her.

If only she could find that pantyhose. Mel tugged open the bottom drawer of her dresser and dug around inside. Sure enough, there were several pairs of pantyhose balled up in the corner. Mel grabbed them, and froze.

Buried beneath all her junk was the silver and sapphire choker with a ring at the front.

Mel's hand hovered over the necklace as she fought the urge to pick it up. It had been weeks since she'd taken it off, yet she still found herself reaching up to touch it, only to find her neck bare. Mel pulled it out of the drawer and held it up before her eyes. Before she knew it, she had unclasped the back and was fastening it around her neck.

Mel looked at herself in the mirror. The ring sat perfectly in the hollow at the base of her throat. The familiar weight of it was comforting.

Mel sighed. After all this time apart from Vanessa, she couldn't help but feel like she had made a mistake. All this had started because Mel had been afraid that Vanessa didn't truly care about her. But hadn't she shown Mel time and time again that she did? It wasn't the gifts and the extravagant gestures. It was the little things. Remembering small, seemingly insignificant details about Mel, like how she loved daffodils and the color blue. Listening to Mel talk for hours while they lay in bed together. Letting Mel see that softer side of her that Vanessa didn't show anyone.

Despite the nature of their relationship, they were always equals. Unlike Kim, Vanessa had respected Mel and her feelings. Vanessa did everything she could to make Mel happy. And that night that she'd told Mel about Rose, Vanessa had admitted that she was falling for Mel.

As Mel fingered the choker around her neck, something that Vanessa had said that night she had given Mel the necklace came back to her. *I'm yours as much as you are mine.* It was all so obvious now. Vanessa had felt the same way about Mel that Mel felt about her.

And Mel loved her.

Mel had been in love with Vanessa for god knows how

long. But fear had kept her from admitting it, even to herself. As she stood there, staring into the mirror, all those fears came rushing back.

No. No more excuses. No more self-pity. Mel steeled herself. Vanessa had always been the dominant one in their relationship. But that didn't mean that Mel was powerless. It was time for her to take control. She hoped that it wasn't too late.

Mel looked at the clock. She needed to see Vanessa, face to face, before she lost her resolve. But it was getting late. And Mel didn't even know where to find her. Unless…

Mel opened her wardrobe and dug out the clutch that Vanessa had given her for the charity fundraiser. In a small pocket in the lining, right where Mel had put it, was a white business card.

Mel picked up her phone and dialed the number.

"Elena? I need a favor."

———

Half an hour later, Elena pulled up at the front of Mel's building. Within seconds, they were on their way to Vanessa's apartment.

"Thank you so much for this, Elena," Mel said.

"Not a problem," Elena replied.

"I wasn't sure if you'd want to help me since Vanessa and I… you know."

Elena shrugged. "It doesn't matter. She still cares about you."

Elena's words buoyed Mel. She didn't know if Vanessa would take her back. But she needed to speak to Vanessa, if only just to apologize, and to tell Vanessa how she felt. She just hoped Vanessa still felt the same way.

"Don't worry." Elena glanced at Mel in the rear-view mirror and shot her a warm smile. "I wouldn't be helping you if I didn't think Vanessa wanted to see you. She misses you."

All Mel could manage in return was a nervous smile. The rest of the car ride passed in silence. When they finally arrived at Vanessa's apartment, Elena parked the car and got out.

"I'll let you into the building." Elena held up a keycard. "After that, you're on your own."

"Thanks." Mel was grateful that she didn't have to ask Vanessa to buzz her up through the intercom.

Mel raced toward the building, Elena on her heels. Elena swiped her into the lobby.

"Thanks again, Elena," Mel said. "I owe you one."

"Any time." Elena gave Mel a farewell nod. "Good luck."

The elevator ride up to Vanessa's apartment seemed to take forever. When Mel reached the top floor, she dashed to Vanessa's front door.

Mel took a deep breath and knocked. Moments later, the door swung open.

"Melanie?" Vanessa stood in the doorway in a silky robe. She had a towel over one arm and her hair was damp.

"Vanessa," Mel said. After all this time, Vanessa was still able to take Mel's breath away.

For a moment, they stood there, on opposite sides of the doorway, their gazes locked.

Vanessa's eyes fell to Mel's neck. Seeing her choker there

broke her out of her trance. She opened the door wide. "Come in."

As soon as Mel was inside, everything spilled out. "I'm so sorry, Vanessa. For everything. I'm sorry that I behaved the way I did. I'm sorry that I said all those horrible things. I'm sorry that I walked away from you-"

"Melanie," Vanessa said. "Sit down."

Mel obeyed.

"You don't have to apologize. I understand."

"No, I do. And I want to explain myself," Mel said. "All my life, everyone I've ever loved has abandoned me. My father. My mother. She would leave me alone or forget about me, time and time again, and she was never really there when I needed her. So, all that time ago, I told myself I didn't need anyone else. I told myself I didn't need love. And after a while, I began to believe it." Mel felt a torrent of emotions rising up.

Vanessa reached out and placed her hand on Mel's.

A sense of calm washed over her. Mel continued. "But you? You made me remember what it was like to feel loved. And it terrified me. The only other person who made me feel like that was Kim. I think she loved me too in her own twisted way. But she manipulated me and toyed with my emotions until I didn't know what to feel anymore. And in the end, she abandoned me too. And she told me she never loved me and that none of what I felt was real. It crushed me. So when Rose came along and said all those things, it reawakened all those doubts and fears. I was scared of getting hurt again, so I pushed you away. And I did it in the most destructive way possible, and I'm so sorry..."

"It's all right, Melanie," Vanessa said. "I understand."

"But that's not all. After everything that happened, I realized that I can't let my past hold me hostage. And I realized that what we had was too precious to give up on. And I realized that I couldn't hide from my feelings. Vanessa—" Mel's pulse was racing "—I love you."

Vanessa smiled. She wrapped her arms around Mel and pulled her in close. "Oh, Melanie. I promise you, I feel the same way. I always have. From the start, I never thought of you as my submissive because I always hoped for more. It took me a while to admit it to myself. I was afraid that if I held you too tightly I'd hurt you like I did Rose. But I couldn't help myself. I did everything I could to make you mine, but I never told you how I really felt. It's the biggest mistake I ever made. So I'm telling you now." Vanessa took Mel's hands in hers. "I love you, Melanie."

Mel's heart sang in her chest. She leaned over and kissed Vanessa, soft and slow, gentle and sweet. Mel had missed those lips. They seemed to fit perfectly with her own.

"It's time we made another rule," Vanessa said. "Next time one of us has a problem? We talk about it. And face it together. No lies, no keeping everything inside. No lashing out. And no disappearing acts. How does that sound?"

"Okay." They had been given a second chance at this. Mel was not going to mess it up. She closed her eyes and nestled in closer to Vanessa, and they sat there together, silent and still.

"Melanie?"

"Yes?" Mel could feel Vanessa's heartbeat pulsing through her body.

"I want to show you my playroom."

CHAPTER TWENTY-FIVE

*V*anessa unlocked the door to the playroom and flicked on the light. Mel followed her inside. She was immediately reminded of The Scarlet Room at Lilith's Den. Was The Scarlet Room inspired by Vanessa's playroom or the other way around? The only difference was that this room seemed more intimate and personal. It was packed to the brim with every toy and tool imaginable, each carefully organized and lovingly cared for. A rack on the wall displayed a collection of whips, crops, and canes, all with crimson leather handles like Vanessa's riding crop. At the end of the room was an elaborate iron four-poster bed with rings all along the frame. Tie points. The smell of leather hung in the air.

Vanessa walked to the center of the room, her bare feet padding on the floorboards. She looked around, an undecipherable expression on her face.

"Are you all right, Vanessa?" Mel asked.

"Yes. It's the first time I've been in here with someone since Rose."

Mel took Vanessa's hand. "We don't have to do this."

"I know." She squeezed Mel's hand back. "But I want to share this with you."

Vanessa pulled Mel in close and kissed her. Mel pressed her body up against Vanessa's, returning the kiss with double the intensity. It had been so long since she'd held Vanessa like this. Vanessa's soft, full lips seemed to melt against hers.

Vanessa pulled away. "Slow down, my pet. We have all the time in the world. And we have all of this at our disposal." She gestured around the room. "Within these four walls, the possibilities are endless. So tell me, Melanie. What do you want me to do for you tonight? What is it you desire more than anything?"

Mel looked around her. The playroom was well stocked. There was so much that she wanted to do with Vanessa. So much that she wanted to try. But right now, she only wanted one thing. "I want you, Vanessa. But I want all of you. I want the dominant, commanding you who can bring me to my knees with no more than a look. I want the sweet, tender you that I saw that night after the fundraiser. I want to serve you. I want to be yours in every sense of the word. But I want to be able to touch you and make you feel the way that I feel when you touch me. I want to see that vulnerable side of you that no one else gets to see."

Vanessa's face wore a strange expression. She pulled Mel over to the bed, and they sat down. "The night that we fought, you said that to me," Vanessa said. "That I kept you at arm's length. That I never gave you any of myself."

"I'm sorry, I didn't mean all of that. I was angry, and Rose's words were in my head, and-"

"It's all right, Melanie. You were right. I expected you to give me your everything when I gave you very little in return. I'm sorry."

"All I want is for you to feel like you can open up to me," Mel said. "Like you can become vulnerable with me."

"I understand," Vanessa said. "I was never good at opening up, and after everything with Rose, I closed myself off even more. I've been that way for so long now that I've forgotten how to let people in. But I want to let you in. I won't hold any part of myself back from you any longer."

Mel smiled. "Thanks, Vanessa. That's all I want."

Vanessa kissed Mel again, hard. Her lips were overpowering. "You also said you want to make me feel the way you feel when I touch you." She drew a hand down Mel's cheek. "How do I make you feel?"

"Like you're my everything," Mel said. "Like I'm the center of your world. Like I'm safe with you."

"I already feel like that, Melanie. But if you want to show me what that's like, I'll let you." Vanessa had a familiar gleam in her eyes. "But we're going to do it my way."

Mel's pulse sped up. In an instant, Vanessa had transformed into the self-possessed, domineering woman who had captured Mel's attention from the first time Mel laid eyes on her. Mel now understood that it wasn't a mask. It was just one of Vanessa's many facets.

"Stand up for me, Melanie," Vanessa said. She waited for Mel to obey. "Take off your clothes. All of them."

Mel began to strip slowly, piece by piece, peering at Vanessa from under her eyelashes. To Vanessa's credit, she didn't break her gaze until Mel stood before her in nothing but the collar around her neck. Then Vanessa looked Mel up and down, drinking Mel in with her eyes. There was a slight chill in the room, causing tiny goosebumps to sprout on Mel's skin.

"There's a blindfold in the chest over there." Vanessa pointed across the room. "Bring it to me."

Mel went over to the chest and dug around for the blindfold. When she returned to the bed, Vanessa had removed her robe and was reclining in the center of the bed, her back propped up on a mountain of pillows. Mel traced her eyes over Vanessa's naked figure unashamedly as she handed Vanessa the blindfold.

Vanessa patted the bed next to her. "Come. Kneel."

Mel hopped onto the bed and knelt beside Vanessa.

The moment the blindfold went over Mel's eyes, Vanessa became her world. She listened carefully to the sound of Vanessa's breath and inhaled the clean scent of Vanessa's freshly washed skin. Mel wanted to reach out and touch her, but she didn't dare to do so without permission.

"So you want to serve me?" Vanessa asked, her voice low and hypnotic.

"Yes, Vanessa. More than anything."

"Then make me feel like your queen. Worship every inch of me. Show me that you're mine."

"Yes, Vanessa." Mel reached toward where she sensed Vanessa was, until her fingertips touched Vanessa's soft skin. She traced her fingers down the length of Vanessa's body and slithered down to Vanessa's feet.

Mel took Vanessa's command to worship every inch of her literally. Mel worked her way upwards, exploring every part of Vanessa's body as if touching Vanessa for the first time. Her lips followed the trail made by her fingertips.

When she reached the insides of Vanessa's thighs, she lingered. Vanessa's scent tempted Mel to taste her then and there. But Mel wanted to draw everything out, to savor every moment, to map every stretch of Vanessa's skin.

She kissed her way up Vanessa's smooth, flat stomach, caressing the other woman's curves with her hands. When Mel drew her hands over Vanessa's breasts, she found that Vanessa's nipples had already formed into tight peaks. Despite the blindfold, Mel could see Vanessa's rosy pink buds clearly in her mind. As soon as Mel's lips touched them, Vanessa's whole body tremored. Mel showered attention on Vanessa's breasts and nipples, reveling in the soft sounds she elicited from deep within Vanessa's chest.

As Mel kissed her way up Vanessa's neck, Vanessa took Mel's face in her hands and kissed her hungrily. "I want you to devour me," she said.

Mel slid a probing hand down between Vanessa's legs. Her fingers slipped easily into Vanessa's silky, wet folds. She crawled back downward, painting kisses down Vanessa's stomach. Mel wanted to take it slow, to tease Vanessa like Vanessa had teased her so many times before. But her own lust got the better of her.

Slowly, Mel parted Vanessa's lips with her tongue and ran it up and down her folds. Vanessa's hands fell down to the back of Mel's head, holding her in place. Mel licked and stroked and flicked away, drunk on Vanessa's taste. Vanessa rocked her hips against Mel's mouth, taking charge of her own pleasure. Muted cries sprung from her lips.

"Melanie," Vanessa said between breaths. "I want you inside me."

"Yes, my Queen." As soon as the words left Mel's lips,

Vanessa's body shivered and her breathing grew heavy. Mel had always been aware of the power Vanessa's words had over her. But until now, she hadn't known that her own words could have the same effect on Vanessa.

Mel slipped a finger inside her, then another. Vanessa gasped, her walls clamping around Mel's fingers. Slowly, Vanessa yielded, and Mel began to dart her fingers in and out. She crawled back up the bed and pressed her body against Vanessa's. Mel wanted to be close to her through this, to dissolve into Vanessa so deeply that she felt everything Vanessa was feeling.

Vanessa let out a low purr as Mel slid her thumb up to Vanessa's swollen nub. Her hands grasped for Mel's body, pulling her in tighter. Mel could feel how close Vanessa was. Finally, Vanessa's body began to quake. Her walls pulsed around Mel's fingers, her wild howl echoing through the room.

Vanessa's scream only emboldened Mel. She thrust away, coaxing out every little part of Vanessa's orgasm. But Mel didn't stop. Another orgasm quickly followed. And another, until finally, Vanessa shattered in Mel's arms.

"Melanie…" Vanessa murmured, breathless.

Mel snuggled into the side of Vanessa's body and threw her arm across Vanessa's chest. Still blindfolded, Mel could feel Vanessa's body slacken and her breathing slow down. Vanessa showed no sign of stirring from her post-orgasm daze.

Mel smiled to herself. This was exactly what she wanted. To give Vanessa everything that Vanessa had given her. To make Vanessa lose herself in Mel and surrender to the pleasure that Mel was giving her. And she had succeeded. More than once.

When Vanessa finally recovered, she pulled off Mel's blindfold. "You served your queen well," Vanessa said. "You've earned yourself a reward." Her lips curved up into a slight smile.

Mel's heart sped up. She knew what that smile meant. Vanessa had relinquished control to Mel, if only for a moment.

Now it was time for her to take it back.

Ten minutes later, Mel was on all fours on the edge of the bed. Her body was positioned so that her ass was thrust up in the air, and her feet hung off the side of the mattress. Her ankles were bound to the bed frame, spreading her legs shoulder-width apart. Her wrists were bound together by a long rope attached to the other side of the bed.

Vanessa double checked her knots, then knelt on the bed in front of Mel. "Now that you're mine again, mind, body, and heart, I'm going to remind you what it means to belong to me." She took Mel's chin in her hands and tipped Mel's face up toward hers. "I'm going to unravel you bit by bit until all that's left is pure unbridled desire, and you're unable to do anything except lose yourself in a haze of ecstasy."

Mel's breath quickened. Vanessa's words alone were enough to make her ache.

Vanessa disappeared somewhere behind her. The position

Mel was in left her unable to see most of the room, so she closed her eyes and listened to Vanessa's soft footsteps. Mel had no idea what Vanessa was going to do with her. But instead of anxious anticipation, Mel felt completely calm. Vanessa knew her deeply. Sometimes it felt like Vanessa knew Mel better than Mel knew herself. And she trusted Vanessa unconditionally.

Vanessa returned to the bed and stood behind Mel. Mel twisted around to look at her. Vanessa held one of her crimson-handled whips in her hand. It was a short flogger with countless leather tails.

"I'm going to introduce you to my favorite toy. It's this flogger here. It has so many uses." Vanessa draped the flogger over Mel's back. "It can be used to tease."

The soft tails of the flogger brushed along Mel's back and down the backs of her thighs. She shuddered with delight.

"With a bit of force, it makes a lovely, solid thud."

Mel felt a firm swat on her bare ass. The impact made her jump.

"Turn it on its side, and it stings just as much as a riding crop." Vanessa whipped Mel again.

Mel hissed. It was like a hundred tiny needles had pierced her skin.

"And once you get into a rhythm, it can be almost hypnotic." Vanessa brought the flogger down on Mel's thrust out ass over and over, one cheek then the other, firmly but not hard enough to really hurt.

"Mmmm..." Mel closed her eyes as Vanessa drew stripes across her skin with the whip. She embraced the sensations, pushing herself out to meet the flogger, losing all sense of time. The next thing she knew, Vanessa was massaging her tender, hot cheeks.

"That was just the warm-up," Vanessa said. "Now it's time for the real thing."

Mel shifted in her bonds, anticipation brewing inside of her. The ropes barely allowed her to move an inch.

"I'm going to flog you ten times. Harder this time. I want you to count them out loud for me."

"Yes, Vanessa," Mel replied.

Vanessa took a few steps back. Mel tensed, waiting for the inevitable. Silence hung in the air. But the flogger didn't fall. After what felt like minutes, Mel relaxed her body.

Slap! Mel cried out. The flogger stung like hell on her already raw skin. But it left behind a pleasant burning feeling.

"Count," Vanessa said.

"One." *Slap!* Mel's fingers curled around the silk bedsheets beneath her. "Two."

Mel continued to count, the heat of the blows spreading across her cheeks and the backs of her thighs. When she reached five, Vanessa slid the flogger down between Mel's legs, teasing her lips with its tails. Mel murmured softly and spread her knees apart as far as she could in her restraints.

Vanessa's response was a sharp, stinging strike.

Mel gritted her teeth. "Six."

Vanessa alternated between stinging lashes and gentle brushes of the flogger against Mel's swollen lips. As the conflicting sensations flooded Mel's body, she found herself slipping into that state of bliss. As soon as the word ten left her lips, Mel closed her eyes and surrendered completely, allowing herself to fall, knowing that Vanessa would be there to catch her. The walls fell back, and the room faded into nothing. The world disappeared. All that remained was Vanessa.

Vanessa removed the ropes from Mel's wrists and ankles and laid her down on the bed. Mel's lips sought out Vanessa's lips, her hands grasped at Vanessa's curves, her body arched toward Vanessa's. And Vanessa's hands were all over Mel's body, seemingly on every part of her electrified skin at the same time. And Vanessa's lips, soft and wet, roamed down her neck, and across her breasts, and over her tiny pebbled nipples.

"Oh god, Vanessa." Mel was drowning in her. "I need you. Please!"

Vanessa pushed Mel's knees apart. The moment Vanessa slipped her fingers inside, Mel crumbled. Her heavy breaths turned into gasps, and her gasps turned into moans. Vanessa's thumb worked Mel's clit while her fingers plunged in and out, her whole body pushing against Mel's with every thrust. Mel whimpered. She felt like she was going to burst.

"Do you want me to let you come?" Vanessa asked.

Mel nodded.

"Then tell me." Vanessa leaned down and spoke into Mel's ear. "Who do you belong to?"

"You, Vanessa," Mel whispered. "I belong to you."

Only then did Vanessa allow Mel her release. Mel cried out as pleasure overtook her. Vanessa held her close, still inside her and all around her at the same time, as she rode out her orgasm like a wave.

When Mel came back down to her body she was wrapped in Vanessa's arms underneath a pile of soft blankets. The floral scent of Vanessa's damp hair hung in the air.

The press of Vanessa's body against hers felt familiar and comforting.

Mel let out a sigh. "This was always my favorite part."

"Mine too," Vanessa murmured. "Every time I put my arms around you, I didn't want to let go."

"You never have to. I'm not going anywhere." Mel said. "I'm yours, after all."

Vanessa kissed Mel softly on the lips. "You're mine," she said. "And I'm yours."

EPILOGUE

VANESSA

*V*anessa awoke in an unfamiliar bed. Sunlight streamed through the window, warming her bare skin. The air was filled with the scent of daffodils. Mel's favorite. Vanessa turned her head to the side. Mel lay next to her, fast asleep. She was still wearing that necklace that Vanessa gave her. She never seemed to take it off.

Vanessa smiled to herself. It was the first day of their island getaway, the holiday that Vanessa had 'won' for Mel at the fundraiser. They'd only just managed to squeeze it in before summer ended. Although they were only here for a few days, Vanessa had a great deal planned, most of which didn't involve them leaving their suite.

Vanessa watched Mel's chest rise and fall. She looked so serene. Vanessa would never get tired of watching Mel sleep. She had almost let Mel slip away. She would never make that mistake again.

Mel's eyelids fluttered open.

"Good morning." Vanessa leaned down and kissed Mel on the lips.

"Mmmm..." Mel closed her eyes again. "What time is it?"

"Late," Vanessa said. "We slept in."

Mel yawned. "I should check my email."

Vanessa nodded. After Mel's summer internship at The LSP, she had been hired part-time as a legal secretary. Her superiors had come to rely on her to the point where they would email and call her even on her days off. But Mel didn't seem to mind. She believed in the work they were doing.

Mel rolled onto her back and scrolled through her phone. After a few seconds, she scrunched up her face, her finger frozen above the screen.

"Is everything all right?" Vanessa asked.

"Yeah. It's fine."

"Melanie." It was clear to Vanessa that Mel was not fine. "No lies, remember? No keeping things to ourselves."

"Sorry." Mel placed her phone down next to her on the bed. "It's a hard habit to break."

"It is for me too. But we can't be solitary creatures anymore." Vanessa propped herself up on her arm. "You don't have to tell me everything. Just know that you can if you want to."

"I know," Mel said. "It's just, I got a message. It's from Kim. She hasn't tried to contact me all this time..."

"What does she want?" Vanessa tried very hard to keep her displeasure from showing. She hated Kim because of how Kim had treated Mel. And the last thing the two of them needed was another ex causing trouble. The first thing that Vanessa had done after she and Mel had gotten back together was take out a restraining order on Rose. She was finally out of Vanessa's life for good.

"I don't know," Mel said. "And I don't want to know. It's all in the past." Mel tapped the screen a few times and set down her phone. "There. I deleted it. And blocked her."

"Are you okay?"

"Yeah." Mel smiled and closed her eyes. "I am. Because you're here."

"Good. I want you all to myself this weekend." Vanessa said. "With all the business trips I've been going on, and work and law school for you, it seems like we barely get to see each other anymore."

"I know. It sucks." Mel yawned and settled in closer to Vanessa. "I don't want this trip to end."

Vanessa thought for a moment. "Well, we can't stay here forever, but I think I have a solution."

"Hmmm?"

"How would you like to move in together?"

"What? Are you serious?"

Vanessa nodded. She wasn't the type to make spontaneous decisions, but this felt right. "You could move into my apartment. Or we could get a place of our own if you'd prefer it. Somewhere new..." Vanessa trailed off. She was unable to read the expression on Mel's face. "What do you think?"

"Yes." A smile spread across Mel's face. "Of course. I would love that, Vanessa."

"That's settled then." Vanessa planted a firm kiss on Mel's lips. Then in one swift motion, she pinned Mel's shoulders to the bed and straddled her body. "Now I can have you all to myself whenever I want. Do you like the sound of that, my pet?"

Mel was definitely awake now. "Yes, my Queen."

Heat rose up inside Vanessa's body. She still wasn't used to Mel addressing her like that. And it was becoming apparent that Mel knew exactly how much it turned Vanessa on.

Mel squirmed underneath her playfully. Vanessa had been gazing down at her girlfriend like a lovesick teenager for far too long. She was getting soft.

And Mel was getting far too bold.

"Don't think I don't know what you're doing. You've been forgetting your place lately." Vanessa reached over to the nightstand and picked up a pair of handcuffs they had used the night before. She dangled them over Mel's body. "Now that we're going to be living together, I'm going to remind you of it. Every. Single. Day."

Mel stopped moving. Her eyes were fixed on the hand-cuffs. *Not so bold anymore, are you?* Vanessa grabbed Mel's wrists and pulled them above her head. She looped the cuffs around a post on the headboard and fastened them around Mel's wrist.

Vanessa got up from the bed and picked up her phone. "Looks like I missed a few work calls while we slept. I should go deal with them." She watched the expression on Mel's face shift from excitement to disbelief. Vanessa only had one call to make. It wouldn't take her more than two minutes. But she wanted to make Mel squirm.

"Are you really going to leave me here like this?" Mel asked.

"Yes. Is that a problem?"

Mel bit her lip. "No, Vanessa."

Vanessa sighed. The look of dismay on Mel's face was almost too much to bear. Vanessa leaned down to give Mel a reassuring kiss. However, as soon as Vanessa's lips touched Mel's, it became clear that Mel didn't mind her predicament one bit.

"Don't go anywhere," Vanessa said.

Mel smiled. "Yes, Vanessa."

ABOUT THE AUTHOR

Anna Stone is the bestselling author of Being Hers. Her lesbian romance novels are sweet, passionate, and sizzle with heat. When she isn't writing, Anna can usually be found lazing around on the beach with a book.
Anna currently lives on the sunny east coast of Australia.

Visit www.annastoneauthor.com for information on her books and to sign up for her newsletter.

 facebook.com/AnnaStoneRomance
twitter.com/AnnaStoneAuthor

CPSIA information can be obtained
at www.ICGtesting.com
Printed in the USA
LVHW090952190921
698201LV00017B/329